I tried all that I could to keep that curse away, but I'm afraid I can't change what has already been written.

Vivian

Chapter 1

Hiding In the Fiction Section

“Woah look at this turnout out” The tone in her voice made it sound like this was her event. There were hundreds of people standing outside waiting, less than patiently, for the library doors to open to get their chance to meet the author who made the town of Grand Fayword a little special. “I haven’t read the book yet, is it really this good?” Charlie’s best friend, Amelie asked, turning her eyes away from the window to look at Charlie.

Charlie shrugged. “The book was good, but I think a lot of the people are here because they think our town is cursed.” Today was the book signing for a book called *Silent Trap*, written by a woman named Sarah L., which was set in Grand Fayword, the name being ironic because the only thing “Grand” about it was the fact that it was a part of this book.

That satisfied Amelie, or she got distracted, because her next comment had her bouncing on her toes. “I know I can’t take all the credit for the amount of people out there, but I think I did a good job for my first real big event.” Amelie had been big into event planning for a while now, she was a part of the high school's STUCO club, and when the girls took jobs as assistants for the local library, Amelie quickly wowed their boss with her ideas for promoting library events. When word got out that the author of *Silent Trap* was making her way back to Grand Fayword, Amelie got a jump on spreading the word and setting up for the event.

Today, in her mind was a test of her abilities. "You did a good job; everything is going to go smoothly" Charlie promised her. "You took care of everything; I don't think I saw you panic once," she said with a small laugh. "Event Planning is your element."

Amelie looked over at her with an excited smile and soon the doors were opened, and a swarm of enthusiastic readers filled the room, making a beeline for the seating area to wait for Sarah L.

The event went smoothly. After Amelie and Charlie had gotten people settled down and Sarah introduced, there wasn't much to do anymore. The two sat on the floor in the fiction section while they waited for the event to end so they could start the cleanup.

Amelie was currently reading *Silent Trap* claiming she could finish the book in time to go speak with the author. Charlie did not doubt her because they had plenty of reading races growing up where they had both found out they were incredibly fast readers.

Charlie had her head resting in Amelie's lap, staring up at the ceiling while listening to the author talk about her motivation for writing, and what had fueled her for this career. It was always interesting to hear how people figured out what they wanted to do in their life, often explaining it was just something they had a passion for, or it was something someone close to them had done. They seemed to always have the answers.

Charlie felt lost, without direction. Amelie had event planning which is something she learned from her mom who was always hosting unique parties at her home. Charlie lived with her uncle, his wife, and their four children. Her mother died when she was young, not knowing much about her besides the stories told to her. Charlie's father left shortly after learning about her mother being pregnant, however, her uncle never hesitated to help his sister out after hearing the news.

For a while, the girl's Aunt Skylar was sweet to her growing up, treating her like one of her own, but when Charlie turned thirteen, it was like a switch flipped. She grew cold, treated her like a built-in housekeeper and babysitter, and talked badly about Charlie's mom when her husband wasn't there. Charlie quickly had to learn how to balance school and being at her aunt's every call, it cost her missing social and other life-changing events. The young girl lost a few friends but was lucky to stay close to the ones that mattered.

"Hiding in the fiction section, is there an underlying meaning to that?" A voice startled Charlie. She looked up and saw that familiar wide grin of her friend Oliver.

Amelie wasn't fazed, not looking up from her book while she spoke. "I guess we didn't hide well enough."

Oliver feigned sadness before sitting down in front of them. "I'm crushed."

Charlie had grown up with these two, meeting Amelie in third grade. She had plopped down next to young Charlie during reading time and given her a pink flower "We're friends now" She had said, and Charlie just went with it. Amelie had always been different than the others, bolder, braver, and always seemed to have the answers. Charlie admired her.

Charlie met Oliver in fifth grade. They had to play soccer in P.E. for a week, she enjoyed playing soccer and figured she was pretty good at it. She still remembers how their coach was calling names for each team; Oliver had come up to her while she sat on the bleachers waiting for her name to be called. "I want Charlie on my team!" He yelled to the coach. From then on Oliver and her survived P.E together, since Amelie had music class. The integration between the three friends went smoothly.

"Why are we hiding out here if this is your event, Amelie?" He knew how deep into her book she was but that didn't typically keep him from talking to her.

"Not my event," She corrected. "I just got the word out and set up the place." She glanced at him "My work here is done until cleanup."

"Well, you got the word out. Probably could've made this place packed even if the book wasn't set in our town."

Amelie didn't reply. Oliver got distracted staring at one of the posters on the walls. Charlie couldn't help but stare at him for a moment, glancing at his grey shirt that had 'I feel like carrot soup' in bold, orange text, it was one of Oliver's own creations. She couldn't remember the exact context but did remember being at Amelie's house. Oliver was complaining about something, got quiet then whispered, "I feel like carrot soup." Whether that meant he wanted to eat carrot soup, or that he felt like a carrot in soup, was never figured out.

He had a creative, odd mind. He had started designing t-shirts and posters of all the odd things the group had said and gifting them to the girls randomly. Charlie's favorite design so far was a pink shirt with a floral design that had a quote from a time Amelie was in a particularly good mood, talking about how great the day had been, and how great they were. The group had been hanging out at the park after school. Amelie had climbed onto the other swing next to Charlie, "We were put on the beautiful earth too..." There was a thud and when Charlie looked over, Amelie had fallen off the swing, "Oh fuck." That had cracked Oliver up and that was how "We were put on this beautiful earth to... oh fuck" was born.

Even Oliver seemed to have things figured out, he wanted to be a graphic designer. During his free time not playing high school soccer, he was perfecting his craft. It was just another example of someone turning their hobby into a career. Compared to Amelie and Oliver, Charlie felt directionless.

"Someone is spiraling again!" Oliver spoke, shaking Charlie from her thoughts. His eyes met hers, tilted his head, and smiled. "I promise whatever you are thinking about is not more entertaining than this…" He reached into his bag and tossed something into her lap.

She picked it up, it being a green bucket hat with the words "I am the collapse of an empire" on it. That made her laugh and look over at him.

He grinned proudly and then nodded towards Amelie, who was still very much wrapped up in her book. Carefully, Charlie sat up and placed the hat on her head, making sure to not tug on her box braids.

"I don't even want to know what it says," says Amelie, not bothering to look up from her book. "I'm not a hat person."

"It's the words of a genius," he said knowing well that Charlie had said that one night when she had gotten sick. "But you are a 'gift from Charlie' kind of person" He retorted.

"Well played." Amelie didn't look at him but at Charlie instead. "How does it look?"

"Are you sure you aren't a hat person?"

She smiled and looked back at her book, "I'm almost done and then we can go check in on everything."

Oliver clasps his hands together. "Great then we can go get something to eat!" He paused for a second then pointed right at

Charlie. "Remind me to give you your sweatshirt. Same quote, I just know you don't like hats."

Charlie was not a fan of hats either. Amelie didn't like them because she didn't think they went with her style. Charlie struggled with hats because they never fit well with her afro, and when she could get them on it didn't feel comfortable and her hair typically took the shape of the hat afterward. Taking the phrase hat hair to a new level.

20 minutes later Amelie had finished up the book and was standing in line to meet the author. Oliver and Charlie were cleaning up a few tables.

"I didn't think Amelie was a big *Silent Trap* fan," Oliver says while tossing a crumpled-up piece of paper into the trash.

"She's been wanting to read it for a while but had to finish up some other books on her lists." Charlie shook her head and ran a rag over the wooden table. "She was just as hyped as everyone else when the book was published."

"You're not going to read it?" he asked curiously.

"I don't want to base my opinion on the fact that our town is the setting. Besides, now people think that our town holds some kind of *curse*."

"Guys! I got the book signed! I can't believe that Sarah used to live here!" Amelie said while making her way back to the group, holding up her copy proudly. "This is why I love our town, so many great people, so many great stories!"

"Great places to eat," Oliver adds.

"Oliver, I will feed you in a second, gimmie a minute." She gestures to the area around her. "The faster you help us clean, the faster we can go."

The three of them finished cleaning up, wiping down tables, and putting chairs back where they belonged. Charlie had just finished vacuuming and met up with her friends who were talking to a blonde woman wearing a black pant suit. She made it to them in time to hear the woman speak.

"Are you Amelie Henderson?" she asked, looking at Amelie. Her head cocked to the side, eyeing her hat. "Nice hat."

"Thank you, I made it!" Oliver said proudly, while Amelie quickly took it off her head.

"I am Claire Carter; I work at Lifestyle Event Planning. I met your mother, and we talked about you and your talents when it comes to event planning," she started. "I heard you are the President of your Student Council?"

Amelie nodded quickly "Yes, I've coordinated a lot of school functions, as well as events for family and friends. I even help when the library hosts events."

Claire nodded "I've seen your posts on social media, and I talked with your boss." She reaches into her bag and hands her a business card. "You have incredible skills for someone your age, your talents are something we need at Lifestyle. Call the number on that card, I'd like you to interview for us."

The next few moments were a blur. Amelie had thanked Claire, then turned to Charlie excitedly after the woman had left. "I might have a job as an event planner!" Her excitement registered in the other girl's brain enough to generate a small smile.

"I heard." Charlie spoke softly. But all she could think of was that she might not be able to work with her best friend anymore.

Chapter 2

Curses & Other Things That Don't Exists

"Are we having this conversation again?" Charlie asked, looking over to Amelie.

"Yes, it's Halloween and relevant," Amelie responded with a big smile. "This is my favorite topic."

It was Halloween in the small town. It had been a week since the author of *Silent Trap* had shown up in Grand Fayword, which was now the current conversation between the girls.

"It's cool that our town was put in a book but come on a story about a nonexistent curse called 'Silent Trap' is a little cliché don't you think?"

"Don't be such a hater, the book is good and I'm glad that Grand Fayword has recognition. I love this place, it's so electric. There are old people here who have stories and new people who are learning what it's all about."

Charlie wondered if Claire Carter was one of the people she was thinking of. They hadn't talked about how her interview earlier this week went. That was fine with Charlie because she still hadn't figured out how to react to this.

Grand Fayword was a big community despite being a small town. Any opportunity to celebrate as a community was taken, that's why even Halloween is a big deal. The girls were dressed up as fairies,

Amelie's green floral, flowy dress and her cellophane film and iron on vinyl indicated she was a garden fairy, on the other hand, Charlie was not a specific fairy, similar pink floral flowy dress, and wings, with flowers strategically placed in her afro.

Oliver hadn't said anything, entertained by a pack of tropical Skittles. He wore a lab coat with jeans and carried a butterfly net. He claimed to be a fairy catcher and spent the first five minutes of their walk putting the net over Charlie.

The leaves tumble on their way to the ground, crunching beneath their feet, the soft loamy earth air rendered damp by the sweet fall rains accompanied by the sounds of the neighbor's trick or treating solidified that this would be a cool, enjoyable Halloween night.

"I'm not a hater" Charlie argued. "I just think it's weird that some people who visit here believe in something like a curse. There's no curse here, the only reason people don't leave here is probably for their own reasons."

Before the conversation could continue, there was a loud voice that shouted. "That curse is real!"

The three stopped in their tracks and turned to see where the voice had come from. Sitting on a rocking chair on the porch of a small house made of grey brick was Vivian Hayes. Every small town had a member who was eccentric and had crazy stories that were almost unbelievable. That was Vivian. Everyone loved Vivian, she was sweet, like a town grandma, just a little kooky. Her smokey grey head of curls blew slightly in the wind, and her slate-grey eyes stared down at the kids, slightly drawing them in.

"What did you say, Ms. Vivian?" Amelie asked politely, walking up to the white picket fence that needed a fresh coat of paint. Charlie had no choice but to follow her, though she did not want to hear any more about this silly curse.

"That curse is real" Vivian repeated. "Now I don't just mean in some silly book, that story made it seem like a hoax, but the curse is real, and you should be worried that it will find a home in you." Her eyes locked eyes with Charlie, sending shivers down her spine.

"Well, how does someone get cursed? Is it the same as in the story?" Amelie asked.

Oh, don't entertain this Amelie. Charlie thought.

"I never read the book, and I don't plan on it." She started. "The curse of not being able to leave Grand Fayword is true. You can walk towards the edge of town but will never be able to pass that welcome sign." She pointed down the road where the entrance of town was. "You will be right back to the edge of town, almost like a force field is keeping you trapped." Her eyes shifted between the two girls, but they seemed to linger on Charlie longer. "The curse finds its home in someone who has no strong will to leave, someone who doesn't believe they have any purpose or reason outside of Grand Fayword."

"That doesn't seem like much of a curse" Charlie scoffs. "If someone doesn't want to leave then why would it be so bad to never have to leave."

Her eyes trained on the girl, making her wish she never said a word. "It's as if the curse teaches you a lesson. You must sit and watch this town change, watch your friends grow old, and move on. You grow older and it makes you wish you weren't so stubborn about wanting things to change." Her voice trailed off for a moment.

"How does someone lift the curse?" Amelie asked softly, sharing a glance with her friend. Vivian seemed to know more than she was letting on.

Vivian sighed slightly, rocking back in her chair. "The only way the curse can be broken is if the cursed one truly wants a better life for themselves, to find more than just what lies here, to find out who they are. Or the curse just finds someone more miserable, more in need of learning a lesson." She looks at Amelie. "What about you dear, what is it you wish for yourself?"

Amelie grinned excitedly; she loved talking about her life plans. "Once I graduate high school, I am going to go to school to be an event planner. I want to be an event planner because you get to meet all kinds of people and get to travel, which I'm excited about. I'm not even worried about some customers being difficult or rude because I have never met a problem I couldn't solve." Her excitement only grew "I didn't tell you, but I interviewed to be an intern at Lifestyle Event Planning."

Vivian was the kind of woman that everyone in town seemed to be drawn too. Amelie, Charlie, and even Oliver had spent some after-school time at her house. Charlie always spent time with Vivian when she was little, the older woman felt like family. She hadn't been around much, between school and taking care of her cousins left little room for free time.

Vivian laughs lightly "You remind me of my best friend Dezi Carver. She was excited about the world, to meet new people" She hummed softly like she was reliving some memories. "She graduated and went on to be a fashion designer. She is doing fabulous things; I believe she is in New York now. Still sends me letters and even some clothes from her current line."

Now Charlie was curious. "How come you don't go see her?"

Vivian looked over at her and was quiet for a second. "What do you plan to do when you graduate?"

This made her feel taken aback. She was seventeen and didn't have a plan. It made her anxious that Amelie, Oliver, and other classmates had a plan of some sort. "Oh, uh well I plan to stay here for college. I have a nice job at the library which I enjoy. I think I want to go to school for Library Science."

Vivian stared for a moment before nodding toward the bucket of candy on the table next to her. "You kids come on up and grab some candy. Don't tell me you're too old for trick-or-treating, you are never too old for candy."

Amelie went first, unlatching the lock and walking up to the porch, followed by Charlie and after she grabbed some candy Charlie did too. Oliver stayed at the gate.

Vivian locked eyes with him, shook her head and threw a piece of candy at him "I don't remember when we started this tradition boy, but I don't mind it."

"Thank you, Ms. Vivian!" Amelie says, returning to the gate, where Oliver had successfully caught the piece of candy and was eating it.

"She didn't ask you what your plan is?" Amelie asked.

"I saw her this morning. I made her a gift" Oliver replied.

Charlie turned to make her way down to the gate but was stopped when Vivian said something.

"You remind me of myself Charlie."

She turned and looked confused. "What?" The words could barely get out.

Vivian didn't say anything else. She just rocked in her chair. "Come on Charlie, we have to show off our costumes!" Amelie called.

Charlie stared at Vivian for a second longer before stumbling down the stairs, hands fumbling with the gate lock. She looked up at Vivian one more time to see her looking towards the edge of town.

Chapter 3

Hear Me Out. You're Wrong

The rest of the night was enjoyable. The three went to some haunted houses, losing Oliver for a moment then found him scaring one of the scare actors, voted on the pumpkin carving contest, tried tons of Halloween treats, and ended the night with the town's Halloween music festival.

Charlie had lost Amelie during the music festival, now she hung on to Oliver while he swung her around, hollering and laughing. As much as she enjoyed the boy's infectious energy, her mind was elsewhere for the rest of the night.

She couldn't fully shake Vivian's comment from her head and when she had gone to bed the old woman's voice echoed in her dreams, waking her up in a cold sweat. She didn't know what it meant but it didn't feel like a compliment.

Now Charlie was sitting on her porch next to Amelie who was trading candy with Charlie's 15-year-old cousin, Victor.

"No, I am not trading my king-sized Hershey bar for 5 measly Reese's Cups." Victor scoffed. "How old do you think I am, five?

Amelie shrugs softly "It did work when you were five. Prime trading time."

Charlie laughed at her comment and Victor's offended face.

"Oh, good there you three are." Uncle Aaron said opening the screen door. "We are going to help Ms. Hayes move."

"Move?" Charlie asked confused.

"Why is she moving? Isn't she like super old? Hasn't she lived here since like… forever?" Victor asked, putting his candy in his bag, swatting at Amelie's hand when she tried to take away a bag of Sour Patch Kids.

"She's not super old, she's 70," Aaron replied. "I am not sure why she is moving but a few of us are going over to help put things in boxes and put them on a moving truck."

Since the weather was warm and Vivian didn't live too far away, they decided to walk. Skylar opted to stay home, claiming she didn't even participate in the moving of her own home so why should she help someone else? Aaron was up in the lead, calling after Victor who was heading the wrong way after he got distracted kicking a rock, but was now running back full speed just to jump on his dad's back.

"Why do you think Vivian is moving?" Amelie asked.

"I don't know. Maybe it's one of those instances where she's got family sending her to an assisted living facility." Charlie shrugged. "It's logical."

"I mean she doesn't seem like she isn't able to live on her own. She was fine during our conversation last night and she always seems fine when I visit her." Amelie shrugs. "The last time I talked to her was because she called and asked my mom if we had any blue paint. She wanted to touch up her door but didn't have any more of the blue she liked. Mom had me run to the store, find the blue paint and when I went to give it to Vivian, I just offered to paint her door for her."

"Why would she want to paint her door? I mean the fence could use a fresh coat too, why not that?"

"I don't know Charlie, but I started painting. She offered me lemonade and she told me about her life and what Grand Fayword used to be like." She thinks for a second. "All I know about her is that after high school she stayed here for college and became a teacher. She lived in that house her whole life."

Now Charlie was even more confused, why did Vivian feel the need to leave a place she had been her whole life? She always seemed content here, which not only made her wonder where she was planning to go but also had the girl convinced that she was moving to an assisted living facility.

When the group got to Vivian's house there were already some people from the community helping load boxes into a moving van. Vivian held a gift basket filled with sweet treats and chatted with a few people. When she saw the kids, she smiled and made her way over to them. Oliver made his way shortly after.

"I was hoping you guys would stop by," Vivian said smiling. "Only a few boxes are left inside the house, but I have some gifts for the kids." She turned and led the group into the house, they followed her up to the kitchen while Aaron moved to the living room to help with the boxes.

Vivian moved to the counter that was empty except for three gift boxes, strangely all the boxes were shades of blue. She picked up one of the blue boxes and turned back to the group "Oliver came here earlier so he already got his, but Victor this one is for you" She handed the young boy the box and when he lifted the lid she continued. "When you used to come over to my house after school you always loved playing with these toy cars. Do you remember?"

Victor grinned and took out one of the cars "Yeah I remember, it was always one of my favorite things to look forward to" he looked up at Vivian "Thank you."

Vivian smiled and reached for a slightly larger, but still blue box, "This one is for you, Amelie."

Amelie takes the box but doesn't open it yet. "I don't need anything Ms. Vivian, I enjoy coming over just to listen to your stories, besides I didn't get you anything."

The older woman shook her head "I don't need anything; you were so sweet coming to listen to my stories and helping around the house. Please, open it."

Amelie opened the box and took out a pastel pink planner and some brightly colored pens.

"For when you start event planning, you're going to need some place to keep track of all your events, and you can never go wrong with bright pens."

"I love it! Thank you!" Amelie hugged Vivian who happily hugged her back.

"Now Charlie," she says grabbing the last box. "When you were younger you used to come read your new library books to me. We'd sit out on the porch and enjoy the new book you picked up that week, and as you got older, I told you stories about my life, and about your mother" She smiled and handed Charlie a small blue box. "You're such a smart girl, and I know you're going to do great things"

Charlie did remember coming over to Vivian's house after school, those visits became less frequent the more she got busy, which always made her feel a bit sad. Vivian was always sweet, looking after her, and the woman knew so much about Charlie's mom. Charlie took the box and opened it. Inside was a small key chain with a wooden acorn. This was a little confusing but before she could ask Vivian about it Victor spoke.

"Is blue your favorite color or something? These gift boxes are blue and so is your front door. What's with that?"

Vivian laughed, "I enjoy the color blue I was told it represents something beautiful, something I like to live by."

"Alright Ms. Vivian," Aaron said stepping inside the kitchen. "That was the last of the boxes."

"Perfect," she says, looking around the house "It's time to say goodbye" She started to walk out of the kitchen, through the living room and outside.

The kids followed her, but Charlie couldn't stop her mind from racing, *why did she give me an acorn key chain?* She gave Victor and Amelie something that made sense to them. "Ollie, what did you get?"

Oliver looked over and smiled "She crocheted me a blanket. Art for Art," he tells her.

He made Vivian things, so his gift from her made sense. Why was she moving after being here for so long?

"Ms. Vivian, why are you moving? I mean you've lived here for a while, where are you going?" Charlie felt compelled to ask standing on her porch and shutting the blue door.

Vivian hums softly and takes a deep breath. "I am going to stay with my friend Dezi, she has an apartment in New York City and when she gets back into town we're going to catch up." She looks at the girl. "I've spent many years here and, in those years, I have enjoyed my life and the lessons I learned, but now it is time for me to embrace a new life. It's going to be a little scary at first, but I am excited." She sighed happily and opened her arms "Come here you kids" She happily engulfed the group into a big hug and slowly let them go "There is greatness in you, I promise."

Vivian went around, hugging the other members of the town, thanking them for all that they had done for her. She walked to the passenger side of the moving van and looked back at the group that had crowded on the lawn by the truck to send her off, "Remember, even the smallest beginnings can lead to great achievements!"

Charlie felt like she was looking right at her when she said that.

She slammed the door shut and the truck started down the road right towards the edge of town and disappeared.

"Why an acorn?"

"Huh?" Amelie's voice carried over the phone, her face now appearing in view.

Charlie dangled the acorn keychain in the camera view "I don't get why she gave me an acorn keychain."

It had been a day since Vivian gifted Charlie an acorn keychain and left Grand Fayword, and the girl's confusion about the gift and Vivian's sudden move had not disappeared. Today had gone by slowly, Skylar had taken her young kids shopping, Aaron was off at work and Victor was somewhere around town with his friend, Charlie was lying on the floor of her bedroom on Facetime with Amelie. Oliver was also here, hanging off the edge of Charlie's bed. His head resting on the ground.

"Did she tell you stories about acorns or something?"

"No? No stories about acorns, I was never given any books about them, I don't even talk about acorns!" She groaned rolling on her back.

"How does one start a conversation about acorns?" Oliver mumbled, which went ignored.

"I don't know Char, maybe it's just a cute little trinket that she saw and wanted you to have." Her face appeared in the camera, eyebrows knitted together, head tilted "Hey... Oliver?"

Oliver just shows up unannounced to one of the girl's houses 95% of the time. Charlie didn't alert Amelie about him being here because it wasn't a big deal. She could understand her confusion about hearing his voice but not seeing him. However, that wasn't really important right now.

"See I thought about that, even Victor said it was some last-minute gift, but I don't think so. I spent time with Vivian too. I just feel like this has something to do with what she told me Halloween night when we visited her." Charlie felt a little hurt that someone she deemed as close to her had given her a confusing gift. The girl was almost always at Vivian's house, she was the first adult she would go to when she needed someone. She was the one who told Charlie about her mom as a kid, and how she grew up. Charlie couldn't hurt her uncle with those kinds of memories.

Amelie was not in the view of the camera anymore, which was not surprising considering the girl couldn't sit still for the life of her. "What did she say?"

"I remind her of herself. Which was chilling in itself but then she moved out of town, I just have a weird feeling."

Amelie popped back into the frame holding a green feathered boa. "I'm sorry Ms. Vivian, the woman who knows so much about the curse said you remind her of herself?"

"Why do you have a feathered boa?"

"Why are you not more concerned about this!"

"I am! That's why I'm talking to you about it!"

"Charlie this goes beyond just an acorn keychain, what if you are cursed? Ms. Vivian, the one who talked about the curse being passed after it either finds a new host or some lesson is learned, just decides one day to go live in an apartment with her best friend in the city?"

"I'm not cursed Amelie," she said already bored of this conversation. "Curses don't exist. Vivian probably just reconnected with Dezi after your conversation with her."

"Or you're cursed."

"Or hear me out. No."

For some reason, her response earned a laugh from Oliver who slid down onto the floor lying next to her "What a compelling argument. Why didn't you both take debate?'

"Fine, if you believe you aren't cursed to live in Grand Fayword forever then let's find out. We will go to the edge of town and see if you pass through."

Charlie scoffed, "Fine, let's go." she stood up, picking up her phone.

"Come by my house though first because I'm trying to clean up my room."

"Fine." Charlie stood up, shoved the acorn in her jacket pocket, and turned to Oliver "Never a dull moment."

The walk to Amelie's house was nothing. The pair let themselves in, knowing Amelie's parents were at work, they made their way downstairs to Amelie's room. The sight ahead was no surprise, art supplies sitting in a pile by her bed, a few books on the ground by the bookshelf, and makeup pallets splayed out on her desk.

"I thought you were cleaning?" Charlie said moving to the bookshelf, to put the books nicely where they should go. Oliver stood in the doorway knowing better than touching anything of Amelie's.

"I was," she stated. "Then I found this feathered boa and wondered if I could do something with it." She put the boa around her neck and posed in the mirror before making eye contact with Charlie "But your curse is way more interesting. Here could you put this in the closet for me?"

Taking the feathered boa Charlie made her way to the closet; she opened the door and noted it was pretty tidy apart from one out-of-place item. "Why do you have four empty bottles of honey in your closet?"

"Who are you, my mom?"

Charlie decided to chalk it up to another art project and put the boa away.

When she turned around, Amelie had organized her makeup pallets and moved the art supplies to her bed. Her backpack was slung over her shoulder. "What? I'll deal with it later. Let's go!"

The walk towards the edge of town was not long. The weather was oddly still warm for October but that didn't bother anyone. Charlie focused on trying to find crunchy leaves to step on while Amelie babbled on about the curse. They passed by Vivian's house, and suddenly Charlie got nervous. Why did she just leave so soon? There was never any talk about leaving and then one day there were moving vans.

"Alright, we are here," Amelie said looking ahead. Rows of trees with fallen leaves stretched far beyond what they could see. The road stretched on until the next town which was a few hours.

"So, Ms. Vivian said if someone is truly cursed, they won't be able to make it fully passed the welcome sign" The old, white, wooden sign that displayed "Welcome to Grand Fayword" in big black letters stood a few feet out. "I'll go first since I know I'm not cursed."

"I'm not cursed" Muttered Charlie.

Amelie walked ahead, passing a few rows of trees and then three steps passed the welcome sign. "See!" She jogged back over towards the group "Okay now you go."

"Wait I want to go!" Oliver pushed in between the girls "If I get a running start, and I am cursed, do you think I'll fly backward?" He gasped and looked over, eyes wide "Human bowling!" He took off running and made it well past the welcome sign. "Dang" he mumbled making his way back.

"This is silly Amelie." Charlie reminded her but realized it would be no use, and Amelie would keep badgering until one of them was proven right. "Fine."

Charlie took a few steps past the rows of trees. She stopped and looked back at Amelie, not sure what she was afraid of, she was going to walk to the sign and rub it in Amelie's face that there was no curse. No problem. She continued and walked to the welcome sign.

She took one step past the welcome sign before realizing she was back next to Amelie.

Chapter 4

Human Bowling

It didn't make sense. Amelie had been able to take three steps past the sign Oliver had bolted past, but Charlie could only take one step.

"No this is crazy." She walked again, passed the first row of trees, to the welcome sign, and one step forward. Right back to Amelie.

She kept going, multiple times. Trees, sign, one step, Amelie. Over and over until she started running at the sign, trees blurred in her vision, and she hit whatever was stopping her, and appeared next to Amelie again, the momentum having her land on her butt.

"I so did not want to be right about this," Amelie said, reaching out her hand to help Charlie up.

"I was right about human bowling though" Oliver whispers in an attempt to lighten the mood. "If we moved closer, we could've been the pins."

Charlie took her hand and stood up but was still in shock. "I don't…But curses aren't real... Why am I cursed?"

Amelie was quiet for a moment. "I don't know. What do they do in movies when people get cursed?"

"Maybe we should go to the library, that sounds like a smart idea," Oliver said.

Charlie didn't have the energy to argue or even comment, she just followed along. The town's library was a cozy, two-story brick building next to the bakery and a little way down from the school. Charlie always enjoyed heading to the bakery and then the library after school, which was half the reason she started working here, but right now was not the time to enjoy the comfortable atmosphere of the library.

Oliver took the lead, not sure who decided that was a good idea. He grabbed a red-covered book "This is the only book I know about curses" He handed Amelie the book with black lettering, *Silent Trap*

This was going to be of no help. Charlie didn't believe in curses, so it never really clicked with her that of course, the library wouldn't have much in the way of solving curses.

Amelie took the book and stared at him, readjusting her backpack straps before speaking. "I don't think the fiction section is going to be much help."

"You think" Charlie scoffed walking to a table sitting down in a chair and laying her head on the table.

Amelie pulled out a chair next to her and was quiet for a moment, which Charlie didn't mind. It was much easier to wallow in her crumbling reality in silence.

"I just checked online about any kind of curse that talks about being trapped in a town. There's nothing but books including Silent Trap" she says typing on her laptop, "Going deeper than just book level, I found nothing, not even newspaper or journal entries about people staying in their hometown for reasons unknown."

"Great," Charlie muttered not lifting her head. Someone placed their hand on her back, she assumed it was Oliver because Amelie was busy typing away on her laptop.

"I think we should go over what we know" She spoke gently rustling around with her backpack.

Charlie lifted her head to see her pull out a notebook, a few pens, and a plastic skeleton she bought from a Halloween store earlier this month.

"Why did you bring that?"

"Listen, I know you're not used to being wrong and that your reality is crashing but don't take it out on Jermy." She placed the skeleton in her lap and patted his head. "Also, I forgot I put him in my bag so if he asks, he's here for emotional support."

"So am I Jermy, so am I" Oliver moved his hand from Charlie's back and grabbed a purple pen from Amelie.

Charlie didn't respond but moved her chair over to see what Amelie was writing.

"So, we know that Ms. Vivian is the only one in town who knows more about the curse than just what was written in the book." She started. "We also know, the curse finds its home in someone who has no strong urge to leave or has a fear of change, which is then used as a punishment until they truly change, or it finds someone else who needs that lesson."

"Do you think the curse moved on to me because Ms. Vivian learned her lesson or because it found me?"

"Good question. Do you think you have a lesson to learn?"

"No."

She blinked. "Well, obviously that's not the right answer."

"Maybe Vivian didn't learn her lesson but when she realized she was free she took the opportunity. Who knows, that's not important right now. Why do you not want to leave Grand Fayword?" Oliver chimed in.

"I don't know," Charlie said with a shrug. "Grand Fayword has a good college where I can get a good education and not have to travel too far. I can graduate and continue my job here at the library and eventually be a Library Director."

"Why do you want to be a Library Director?" Amelie asked curiously.

She turned to her with eyebrows raised. "Because I get to spend my time in a *library*" She emphasized the word library. "Library Directors typically make really good money and again, it's a *library*."

Amelie shakes her head "I'm not hating on the library but why not work in any library? Why just the one here in town?"

"It's within walking distance from my house, it always smells like sweets from the bakery next door, and I already know everyone who works here."

"You know most libraries have bakeries inside the store, right?"

"Yeah, but there's no guarantee I'll be within walking distance, and I definitely will have to get to know my coworkers."

"But getting to know new people is so fun! I'm sure no matter what library you work at there will be people like you, interested in the same things, that you'll get along with."

Charlie shook her head "That's not really a motivating factor." She gently started to roll one of her pens back and forth against the table. "Being a Library Director is as much fun to me as an event planner is to you, you don't care where or what event you're planning, but I like knowing where I'm staying."

Amelie watched the pen roll back and forth for a moment.

Oliver looked up from the art project he was creating on his arm, "Why not move to Seattle?"

Charlie's brows knitted together, and she blinked slowly. "Why would I move to Seattle?"

"To see The Bean."

"Chicago," She corrected.

"Oh, Chicago is nice too."

Both girls made eye contact and Amelie rolled her eyes before speaking up again. "I think you're cursed to be here because you don't realize the potential you have. You are settling for your hometown for a job you've had since the beginning of high school."

"So, people aren't allowed to not want to move? And I thought you weren't hating on the library." Charlie countered. "Sorry I didn't get an internship." Her voice was low as her eyes went back to the pen.

If the words hurt her, Amelie didn't show it. "I'm not. The difference is that you aren't leaving out of fear. You don't like what you can't control and having no control scares you. That's why I haven't mentioned my interview with you. You don't want to think about not working with me anymore." She paused; Charlie avoided eye contact. "You know where everything is in this town, in this library you know exactly where everything goes, and everything has its system. Past this town, is unknown and that scares you."

Amelie wasn't wrong, and Charlie wouldn't hesitate to agree either. She loves it here because it's familiar. The girl hated that there was a chance that her best friend wouldn't be working with her anymore. Here at her job, everything has a place, and she knew exactly what to expect. "Yeah, now that I think of it, the curse has no downsides."

Amelie and Charlie started their walk back to Charlie's house. Oliver had to go home for dinner. The girls were both quiet, which was a first. Usually, Amelie was rambling on about some story, or some invention that she could totally invent and sell for millions, but this time she said nothing. It was odd. Charlie was used to being the one who stayed silent, enjoying the comfort of her friend's babbling which led her to wonder what all went on in her head.

Charlie glanced over at Amelie, her eyes were down on the ground watching the leaves as she tried to find the crispest one to crunch under her feet. She was biting her bottom lip in between her teeth, Charlie knew that meant she was thinking, and she hoped that her thoughts weren't about the curse, but she knew that it was, knew Amelie wanted to solve this problem, even though Charlie had insisted she was fine with it. There wasn't anywhere she wanted to be, being here was just fine.

When they got to the house, Charlie was the first to the porch steps, holding the door for Amelie. Instantly the room was overpowered by the smell of warm, broccoli cheddar soup. Aaron peaked his head around the corner from the kitchen as the two made their way through the living room "Good you're here, dinner will be done soon" he smiled over at Amelie "Are you staying for dinner?"

Amelie nodded "Yes. It smells good too, can't wait." Amelie was a regular at dinners, her parents often worked late most nights, so Aaron always made enough for Amelie to take home for later.

Amelie and Charlie walked through the living room and up to Charlie's bedroom, where she kicked off her shoes and flopped down on her stomach on the bed. Amelie shut the door behind her, her bag and shoes were taken off and placed next to the nightstand. She sat on the ground leaning against the bed.

“What are you going to do if you get bored here? I mean being cursed here means staying here, for like, ever.” She said looking over at her friend.

Charlie let out a breath while sitting up, “I don’t think I’ll get bored. I mean I enjoy the things I’m doing now. I enjoy going to the bakery after school and I enjoy my work at the library. I enjoy the people because I know all of them already.” Pausing for a moment before she spoke again “I know Ms. Vivian said having the curse would be hard, we don’t even know if she was cursed but if she was, she still made the most of it you know? She was the town’s favorite. She always had stories and went to every event.”

A slight frown deepened on Amelie’s lips, and a soft chuckle escaped them “You know I am going to do everything in my power to keep you from being cursed right?”

Charlie knew that, but she also knew there was nothing anyone could do.

“I know Amelie.”

“We have a week off school which I will dedicate to finding a way to end this curse.”

“I know Amelie.”

She was quiet for a moment. "Because you deserve more than just a simple life in Grand Fayword."

Charlie couldn't agree with her there.

Chapter 5

Strongly Disagree

True to her word, Amelie spent the last two days trying to find ways to break the curse. She did most of her research alone, but when they were together, she asked if Charlie remembered anything from Vivian's stories or if her mind had changed about not wanting to leave.

It hadn't.

Now Amelie, Oliver, and Charlie were sitting comfortably at a table in the back of the library. Amelie had brought a few notebooks, colored pens, and her laptop which she had been silently typing on for a few minutes now. Oliver hadn't brought anything but his sense of humor. Charlie knew he cared about this situation but also knew that he tended to cover things up with jokes and weird conversation topics.

Charlie brought the keychain that Vivian had given her. She stared at it, gently swinging it side to side trying to figure out why Vivian had given this to her. It wasn't like the two weren't close, Amelie might have visited more often than Charlie had as they grew older, but Vivian still watched Charlie grow up, and even before the move she still visited. Charlie couldn't deny the hurt she felt at the gift she was given.

"Here," Amelie said sliding her laptop over.

On the screen was a website with a light pink background and black lettering that said **Personality Test** at the top. "A personality test?"

She nodded. "It will give you careers, strengths, and weaknesses based on the results, which I will use to figure out some kind of motivation to get you out of this town."

Charlie frowned slightly "Ame, I've taken personality tests before and they all talk about how my personality type thrives in noncompetitive, non-high-pressure jobs, jobs that help people. Social worker, teacher, librarian."

"I'm not focusing on your careers right now Charlie, I want to find out more than just what you're not telling me. I know that your job here is not what is holding you back." She points to the laptop "Just… humor me, okay?"

"Fine" she whispered. She focused her attention back on the screen and answered the question based on an "agree" to "disagree" scale. Usually, Charlie loved personality tests, and she loved answering questions to learn more about herself, but somewhere along the line, it got unhealthy. She found herself relying on some stupid tests to tell her who she was, what she liked, and disliked, and what career she **needed** to be in. She needed to know who she was.

Sometimes the questions mocked her, no she didn't regularly make new friends, yes, she made backup plans for her backup plans, the smallest mistake could make her doubt her abilities, yes, she worries too much about people's impressions. What is wrong with her?

Charlie knew that the answer wouldn't be there. She knew what was waiting. The answers she already knew. God, she based her whole career off these stupid tests with their stupid answers that called her out. The screen loaded her test answers, she is reliable, observant, and hardworking, tends to take things personally, represses feelings, and is reluctant to change.

She scrolled down a bit and read about career paths. Librarian was at the top of the list, followed by teacher, social worker, and human resources. She didn't know how to feel as she slid the computer back to Amelie, she wanted to make a snarky remark about how she was right, but decided against it, so she just sat there and watched Amelie read over the results.

Oliver leaned over to read the personality type "ISFJ-T, I think I got ENFP-A" He grinned. "Said I was a free spirit."

Oliver really was something of a free spirit. Charlie didn't know how he always managed to be so optimistic. He was the middle kid with three brothers. Each brother was always in some kind of sport, and even though Oliver enjoyed soccer he had an interest in the arts. Something his father didn't understand, but his mother encouraged.

Amelie was quiet for a moment and nodded softly. "This is pretty accurate. You're loyal, hardworking, reserved, and responsible." Her eyes met with Charlie's "Do you like working at the library? Or are you just playing the part because the test said so?"

"I like working there," she tells her. "I'm good at what I do, I have fun."

Amelie nodded softly and looked back at the screen then back hesitantly "Charlie I can't understand why you don't just want to take a librarian job elsewhere. Or use your college experience to explore other options, maybe a fun hobby to get you out and traveling?"

"Because I don't want to? I'm content with my plan."

"Charlie I am trying to help you here. Why won't you just work with me?"

"Why do you care so much about my life choices? Why can't I just stay here?" Her tone stayed quiet since they were still in the library, but she started to grow annoyed and tired. Amelie had spent days trying to "figure her out" and was coming up empty. It was better to just drop it.

"I am not staying here Charlie!" Amelie spoke in such a way that grasped Charlie's attention without screaming at her. "I'm leaving after high school, you know that. Being upset that I'm not working here at the library anymore is one thing. But you wanting to stay here is another. You are acting like it's no big deal if you're cursed to be here forever, like it won't hurt you to be apart from me" She whispered that last line.

A momentary pause hung in the air, and Charlie's brow furrowed in concentration as she started to connect the dots. Amelie wanted to leave town and had plans to travel because it was something she had always wanted to do. Charlie had focused on the fact that her job was here, her routine was here, and she didn't think there was a big reason to leave. Being cursed here would limit the girls' visits more and more. It would be Amelie always traveling.

Charlie's mouth opened but couldn't get the words to come out. Couldn't tell her best friend that she would miss her, that being stuck here would suck because she would need her.

All she could do was watch Amelie pack up her bag and walk off.

Chapter 6

Engineers and Artists

Charlie's Thursday was spent the same way she had spent the Wednesday night after getting back from the library, lying in bed. She was snuggled under three blankets, headphones on over her ears playing sad music so she could try and figure out her feelings. She was never good at that, and she missed Amelie already; knowing she was frustrated with the situation. Charlie didn't know why it took her so long to understand why Amelie had been so desperate to break this curse. Thinking she was just trying to get Charlie to have a better job than just a librarian, and that she was trying to get Charlie to move up in her life since she was taking her own next steps.

Her thoughts of Amelie and Vivian continued to take the lead in her head when she caught something out of the corner of her eye. She sat up taking her headphones off seeing Amelie shutting the door behind her.

"Hey," she says softly, sitting her bag down.

"Hi," Charlie's voice was barely a whisper, hands grabbing her phone to pause the music.

"Vic let me in" She moved to the bed sitting on the edge of it, looking at her. "I know it's harder for you to process things, so I figured I'd give you a minute."

Charlie nodded thankfully. "I'm sorry Amelie, I wasn't thinking that being stuck here meant losing you."

"I know Charlie, you don't have to apologize. I know you're so used to your routine that you weren't thinking about me leaving."

All she could do was nod again "You're a part of my routine. It was bad enough thinking you might have a new job."

"I know and you weren't focused on that part cause it's always been us" She was right about that. Amelie had always been a constant, never once did Charlie have to worry about them being apart. "But Charlie I have to figure this out. Will you please answer me honestly?"

There was a moment of hesitation before she nodded.

"Do you like working at the library? Or are you just playing the part because the test said so?"

The girl was quiet for a second, trying to think fully about the truth of her actions. She liked working at the library and enjoyed what she did there. But what made her decide to work there?

After a moment she had an answer. "Yes. The test said it would be a good fit, so I looked into the career of library director and thought it sounded good. I got a job here to test myself in the environment."

"Thank you." She sighs. "But you know you don't have to just be a library director because of some test results, you don't have to continue working at a library just because the environment is good, you can go out and explore other options."

"No, I can't" She interrupts her, now noticing the way she tilted her head and decided to explain before Amelie wasted energy asking why. "I don't have any other idea what I want to do. Not everyone was born with a passion like you." These thoughts were reoccurring. Charlie wasn't jealous of much, but she was jealous of those who knew what they wanted to do. Who came into this world with a passion, an idea of what they wanted. People wanted to be doctors, engineers, and artists, they found it easily. Charlie was just here following the rules. Schooling for multiple years and then a good enough paying job. She didn't have to love it, she just had to do it.

Amelie seemed to be choosing her words carefully, she was good at that. She always spoke without judgment. "Well, let's get off careers for a second. Ms. Vivian said that to break the curse you have to want to leave, some kind of longing for something better" She thinks "Do you have a hobby you like? Something that makes you happy?"

Charlie let out a laugh at that. She didn't mean to, but she had tried to figure this out herself as well. She wasn't skilled like others. Tried to write but her stories sounded choppy, couldn't draw, and didn't understand painting, it has rules but no rules. She wasn't crafty. "I've tried," she says. "I don't have a calling."

"But you have a purpose here."

A frown deepened on her face, and her jaw tightened. "Stop! Please stop! I am so tired of hearing that I have a purpose and that I am more than just ordinary! I can't find it! I don't! I don't!" She sat up on her knees but couldn't manage to look her friend in the eyes. "Everyone has a purpose, everyone was put here to do something, but I can't think of anything that gives me that passion. The most I offer here is helping people. I'm the one people go to for advice, I am always first to help. People say I'm helpful. But you talk about event planning and you deep dive into the interesting aspects of it. Victor finds random topics to research, he knows everything. I don't even know how he figures out *what* exactly to research. Oliver is always coming up with designs like it's easy." Tears threatened to spill, and she choked on her words. "Even Ms. Vivian had a purpose. She might've been cursed here but she had stories. She had *something.*"

Charlie had nothing.

"I tried my best to not worry about it. I figured I would figure something out" She continued to speak for fear that if she stopped it would be hard to start again. "Then it hit me when you got that interview. You are taking your next steps, and I don't have a purpose."

"That's not true Charlie."

She waved her arms and nodded. "It is. I didn't get lucky enough to grow up with opportunities. I would be wonderful if I wanted to be a stay-at-home mom" She refused to make eye contact knowing she looked sad, pathetic even. "Skylar only ever taught me how to cook, clean, and take care of her kids. If I did a sport, I had to be perfect at it or it wasn't even worth doing. Hobbies are a waste of time unless you can turn them into profit" Her hands rubbed against her sweatpants trying to keep herself from panicking. "You're going to move on, have a better job, be a better person and I'm going to get left behind."

Charlie already felt left behind. People her age had been going to parties, and experiencing things normal kids should be experiencing. She only knew how to take care of kids. Kids that started to grow to resent her for the parent role she was thrown into.

Her body felt tired as she sat back on her knees and hung her head. The bed dipped more and soon Amelie was hugging her close. She pulled her in, and Charlie leaned in and cried.

If I were an artist my sadness would be beautiful.

Chapter 7

Moments with Ms. Vivian

"It's weird to me that all of my friends are into things like going to concerts and other social events, but I don't like them."

It was a warm Saturday morning. Fifteen-year-old Charlie was sitting on Vivian's porch. The older woman sat in a rocking chair just listening.

"Do you not enjoy those things or were you not given a chance to experience those things and make a decision for yourself." She replied gently.

Vivian was the only one besides Amelie and Oliver who heard everything about Charlie's family situation. She knew that Skylar had used her as her built-in babysitter. A third parent. Aaron was none the wiser because he worked all day every day until night when everyone had gone to sleep. Vivian had often reminded Charlie to not blame Aaron, he didn't know what was going on, and he would never know if she kept choosing not to tell him.

She refused to tell him, not wanting to cause a fight, and be kicked out of the only place she had to call home. Or worse, she didn't want Aaron to agree with Skylar. Agree that Charlie was only good at being someone else's helper.

Vivian's wise words played in her head. She liked hanging out with Oliver and Amelie, loved it actually. She was always looking forward to being with them, in a group setting or just one on one. With them is where she always had the most fun, the kind of feeling that started in her chest and made her smile so much, the feeling that rushed through her body and made her want to scream with joy and jump around.

She wondered if that was the kind of feeling people felt when going to concerts. If that was true, there was no need to replicate it. "I don't think I ever need to go to concerts. I like staying off to the sidelines."

"Why is that?" Vivian asked.

"I don't know. I still have fun with my friends, I just don't think I need to be a part of the action to have fun" Charlie waited for Vivian to say something but when the woman stayed silent, she continued. "I guess I'm just worried about making a fool of myself." She spoke slowly.

"How could you make a fool of yourself?"

"I don't like having the attention on me, it makes me feel awkward." She mumbled, "I guess it's because Skylar always pointed out every wrong thing I ever did." She filled the silence Vivian gave her to continue to explain "Anytime I messed up she just laughed at me. She always tried to put me down in front of my friends or even sometimes to Uncle Aaron."

Vivian scoffs "Skylar was always a mean girl. Even in high school" She shakes her head "You know your friends aren't paying that close attention to you. They aren't waiting for you to slip up so they can make you the butt of their joke."

Charlie raised her eyebrow "How do you know that?"

"I just do," She says simply "People who care about you don't care even if you do mess up" She looks down at her. "You should go out and do new things. I'm not saying start with a concert but do something fun with your friends. Start a bucket list of things you haven't had time to do because of school and what Skylar makes you do."

"Why?" Charlie asked confused "Usually when people get older, they don't have time with their friends."

"For some people that is the case. However, that is part of the reason I encourage you to try and get out there" She rocked back in her chair slowly. "Go bowling or something. Just enjoy being around your friends. Soon enough you'll have school and your job to focus on and you'll miss the days when you had free time."

Charlie stayed quiet for a moment before looking over at Vivian "What did you do when you were a kid? For fun?"

Vivian was quiet for a moment, rocking slowly in her chair "I didn't do much, I worked a lot, studied" She looked at Charlie and held out her finger, knowing that girl was about to sass her "But, when I did get dragged out, Dezi and I had sleepovers. Went to the movies. Simple but fun things like that"

Charlie accepted that as an answer, nodding her head before looking ahead of her "Sometimes, I feel" She hesitated never having the right word for it "My brain just seems like it doesn't work like others" She could feel Vivian's eyes on her but continued due to the silence. "I can't really explain it, but I know it'll just be classified as different, and people always say being different is a good thing."

"You don't think it is?"

"I do" She paused "But I don't think that having to readjust how I see the world and act in it, is a good kind of difference. I mean I shouldn't get punished for trying to fix something that doesn't work for me."

"Like?"

Charlie rolled her eyes slightly while leaning back against the door. "For instance, I hate that I have to pretend to act a certain way. You know that saying, treat others how you want to be treated? I got in trouble with Aaron one time because I was rude to one of the neighbor kids. But they had been mean to me, so by that rule they treated me how they wanted to be treated, right?" She didn't wait for an answer "And more so, it's so hard to act like a fake person. I hate how I must have facial reactions for people to think I'm listening. I don't have to smile and go above and beyond for you to know I'm paying attention."

"Do you do that often?"

"Not with Amelie or Oliver," she says slowly "But at school, with other people. I've learned that I need to put in more energy, and it feels forced" Charlie turns to look at the woman "So a few days ago someone was talking to me about a movie they had watched, and I wanted to just respond with 'That sounds really cool' because it did! But that doesn't really fly so instead I went like this" Charlie smiled, her eyes went wide, and she had more fluctuation to her voice "No way! Honestly, that sounds really cool" Her face fell back to her normal resting position, and her tone fell flat. "It gets tiring."

"I can see why," Vivian says softly "For the record, I think you're doing a good job at pretending, but you know you don't have to."

Charlie scoffs slightly "If I don't, I'm considered rude."

Vivian just nodded "Keep Amelie and Oliver close to you dear," she says gently. "They won't make a fool of you."

Chapter 8

Moments with Ms. Vivian

"What is love like Ms. Vivian?"

The older woman laughed softly, her eyes following her hands that were gently crocheting something, unrecognizable yet. "Why do you ask Charlie?"

Charlie wasn't sure why she wanted to know. "Was my mom ever in love?" She didn't know anything about her parents' relationship, except for the fact that it couldn't have been good considering her dad left when she was young. She believed Aaron and Skylar were in love, but she wasn't sure she knew the requirements for being in love.

Vivian was quiet for a moment "I suppose she was," the woman said softly. "She had come up to my house one day after school." A small smile on her face appeared as she quoted Charlie's mom "Ms. Vivian, I'm in love" Vivian laughed "She was about sixteen I suppose, and this was the first instance she had ever mentioned a boy, let alone being in love"

"Was she talking about my dad?" Her voice grew curious.

She shook her head, "This boy was named Grayson… Grayson something," she murmured "I can't remember, but he was a respectable young man. Dressed sharply, smart, acted older than his age. I believe that's what attracted your mother. Him being mature for his age."

She looked at the older woman wanting her to continue.

"Your mother often came over, complaining about how all the boys at school were ridiculous and annoying. I understood that very well, you can't be a teacher and

not have your fair share of rowdy boys," she continued "but one day this new kid moved to town and her perspective changed."

Boys were annoying and Charlie couldn't stand them. She could never get interested in who her classmates believed was the most attractive guy and the gossip that went around school. "Did Grayson become her boyfriend?" Charlie knew she should be asking about her father, but Vivian was always careful with what she said regarding her mom, and her father was one topic she usually brushed past. Besides, Charlie found herself wanting to hear more about her mom being in love, she liked picturing her when she was young. Were they the same?

"Oh, he did. The two of them came over after school often. I watched him tutor her in the subjects she struggled with. He walked her to school and home. He went to family dinner, and she even brought him here to have dinner." She was still crocheting, pulling the hook towards her body to tighten it before starting a new pattern. "The boy had come to me second to ask permission to ask out your mother. I always told her 'Lily, you deserve the love you give because you're always putting in 110%."

Charlie was quiet for a moment. In all the stories she was told about her mom, from Vivian, and Aaron, she was always a good person. She was kind, vibrant, and adventurous. Never met someone she couldn't be friends with.

"What happened to them?" Her voice was soft, afraid to destroy the imagery of her mother being young and in love that Vivian had described, but almost longed to know what happened between the time her mother met Grayson and Charlie's existence.

Vivian seemed to hesitate for a moment, almost like she was choosing her words carefully. "They dated throughout high school and college. I watched them grow, their relationship truly was something else, it was everything I wanted for her. They were good communicators and had good boundaries. They loved each other fully." She paused for a moment and glanced at the young girl before going back to her crochet project. "But that made the breakup even more devastating. They graduated college and planned to move in together, said it didn't matter where they were they just wanted to live together. But family has a funny way of changing things."

"What do you mean?"

"Well Grayson's parents were divorced, he had moved here and lived with his mom, but apparently the arrangement had always been that when he got older Grayson would move back to the city and take over the business for his family."

"Why didn't mom go with him?"

"Your grandparents had a struggling business, they needed both your uncle and Lily to help stay afloat." She paused for a moment "Well, that's not entirely true. Your grandmother was supportive of Lily moving out and starting her own life, but your grandfather was determined to keep the business going, especially because it was passed down from his father. Your uncle was also determined to follow in his father's footsteps, and both of those influences kept your mother here."

She frowned softly and shook her head a bit "Okay but why didn't Grayson stay here? Did he even want to run the business?"

Vivian let out a short laugh "Grayson did not want to follow his father's path. He was adamant that he would stay with Lily even if they had to live in the street." She continued. "But he came to me one night frustrated. He had told his mother that he was going wherever Lily was and that he didn't want to leave her or take over the family business. His mother supported him, but she did remind him of the requirements of his father's will. He needed to be ready to take over the business in order to receive any money." Vivian's tone of voice changed to something that Charlie couldn't quite place. "Now Grayson was not materialistic by any means, but his mother reminded him of how hard it was for them when they first moved here, she told him that Lily didn't deserve that."

"What did you tell him?" She hoped that Vivian had tried to convince Grayson to stay, to fight for Lily.

"I didn't tell him anything. That boy loved your mother more than life, and the thought of her having anything but the best didn't sit right with him."

"He took the job."

Vivian nodded. "It was a brutal goodbye," she says quietly. "They spent the whole day together, and when it was time for him to go, I watched that girl follow the truck until it disappeared out of town through the forest. He was yelling at her from the truck window that he loved her and made promises of coming back." Vivian was looking out the window, and Charlie imagined she was replaying the scene that played out right in front of her house.

Charlie thought about Grayson and her mom being in love. Him leaving to go work with his dad. Her mom stayed and worked with her family until her parents passed away. Charlie knew the siblings kept the business together until mom passed away too, then it had become too hard for Aaron, and he had to close down.

Charlie never wanted to love so hard just for it to disappear.

Vivian spoke again, shaking the girl from her thoughts "She stayed out there for a while before I could finally convince her to come inside. She told me she would never love that hard again because it hurt."

"I wouldn't either." Charlie agreed.

'Baby, I'm gonna tell you what I told your mother. If it hurts, that's how you know you loved hard."

Chapter 9

A LEGO Convertible & Some Stairs

Knight Household

Oliver picks up the light blue sweatshirt and lays it flat on the lower plate of the heat press. His hands carefully glided over the material to smooth out any wrinkles. He picks up the printed transfer paper with the quote “I can’t hear you over the sound of how successful I am” on it. He remembered the day well.

Charlie and he were together at his house, building Lego sets. He had an Architecture Eiffel Tower set and Charlie had LEGO Creator Red Convertible. They were heading downstairs to set them with the other LEGO sets in the basement when Oliver jokingly commented on how she had finished faster than he had, she playfully said “I can’t hear you over the sound of how successful I am” before promptly tripping and almost falling down the stairs.

The Red Convertible flew in the air and landed on the floor, half of it still intact. Oliver had reached out and grabbed Charlie, so she didn’t eat it on the stairs. He had dropped his creation but at that moment he didn’t care. After he made sure she was okay, the two of them sat at the bottom of the stairs and put the Red Convertible back together.

That memory made Oliver smile as he placed the transfer paper down on the spot in the middle of the shirt. He carefully closed the heat press lid, then went and sat in his desk chair. He watched the timer count down on the heat press and thought back to that moment when the three of them were at the edge of town. How Charlie had run only to end up right back where she started. He didn't believe in the curse either, but now with proof, he really couldn't dispute it. He didn't think that Charlie was cursed for wanting to work at a library or go to school here. He felt like there was more to it than that.

"Someone is in deep thought," A voice said, "Is it your creative mind turning?"

Oliver looks up to see his mother standing in the doorway. "Oh yeah, just thinking."

His mother, Jamie, glanced over at the heat press and then back at her son "What do we got going on over here?"

Oliver couldn't help the grin that spread across his face. As if on cue the timer beeps, and Oliver strolls over to the machine to lift the lid. He carefully peeled away the transfer paper, revealing the vibrant design now attached to the sweatshirt. Proud with the result, he turns it over to show his mom.

Jamie's eyes ran over the words and a small smile appeared on her face "You made something else for her?" The way her son's face turned red answered the question for her.

"I don't think I'm going to give her the other one I made," he said rubbing the back of his neck before carefully placing the shirt on the table to take to Charlie later.

"The empire shirt? Why not?"

Oliver just shrugged "I think this one is better."

Jamie studied her son, her gaze trailing over to the shirt he just made, then over to the iPad that she knew was filled with designs. No doubt in her mind that the majority of them were for Charlie. "How is she?"

Oliver took a seat on his bed and thought for a moment, there was no way he could tell his mom what had been going on. *'Oh, she's good, you know just dealing with being cursed to live in Grand Fayword forever* sounded" totally normal and not worrisome for a parent at all, he thought.

"She's good." He says after a moment.

"I heard what happened." She met her son's gaze and nodded slowly "Amelie's mom told me that Amelie and Charlie got in a little tiff over careers and life."

Oliver's shoulders relaxed and he ran his fingers through his hair with a small nod. He shouldn't have been surprised that his mom and Amelie's mom, Angela, talked about the kids. They had been friends due to the abundance of playdates Oliver begged his mom to take him to. He enjoyed hanging out with Amelie and Charlie, so he was relieved when his mom got along with their mothers too.

Oliver often thought about the nights that Charlie and Amelia stayed the night at his house or when he and Charlie had gone to Amelie's.

He learned later in life that Jamie and Angela had been taking turns hosting sleepovers and playdates to help Lily with Charlie while she worked.

"I know it must be hard for her," Jamie said softly "I can't even imagine how she's feeling."

Oliver let out a slow breath. "Amelie is trying her best to get Char to want the best for herself" she shrugs "Amelie is moving after college, and she might be a little upset that Charlie isn't seeming that upset about it." Oliver was just assuming but he had grown up with the girls enough to know their personalities. Charlie hardly showed the emotion she was feeling and had a hard time realizing that other people wanted her to show those emotions. Amelie always showed emotion, sometimes a little too hard. Oliver was the mediator most of the time. He would try and remind Amelie that Charlie just expresses her feelings her own way. He would remind Charlie that Amelie wasn't upset with her and was just more expressive at times.

"You know Charlie's always been a little more reserved."

Oliver nodded in agreement.

Jamie takes a deep breath. "I wish Lily, and I hadn't fallen out of touch for so long."

Oliver looked up, his eyebrows knitting together, head tilting lightly. "What do you mean?"

Jamie takes a moment before walking over and sitting next to her son. "I knew Lily in college" She grinned slightly "We were roommates actually."

"I didn't know that. I thought you guys met when Charlie and I met in fifth grade."

Jamie shook her head. "Nope. Lily and I were friends way before then."

"What happened?"

"Lily was very talented" Her head tilted to the side, and she looked down at her hands. "She had her life all planned out. I was by her side through all of it" She went quiet for a moment and closed her eyes. "But life has a funny way of changing things. She met a man, who changed all of that. Or convinced her that she needed changing" She opened her eyes and pushed back her hair. "I tried to talk her out of certain decisions, but I think... I went too far because she stopped talking to me."

Oliver opens his mouth to speak but stops, realizing he didn't have anything important to add. He stayed silent hoping she could continue.

Jamie gathered her thoughts and spoke again. "She came to me one day while I was at home. She carried the cutest little baby with her. Lucky for me I had my own little baby," She ran her hand through his hair and nudged his shoulder. "We sat and talked about our babies and life" Jamie paused for a moment, her eyes shifted back and forth, contemplating how much she should say. "Life got busy for me with your brothers and her with work and we were reunited when 10-year-old Ollie came bounding through the door talking about the coolest girl in P.E. class" she laughed softly.

Oliver laughed with her and smiled fondly back about that day. "Do you..." he hesitated "Do you ever wish that you reached out sooner?"

Jamie's lips pressed together in a straight line, occasionally parting as if she might speak but then closing again as she continued to think. Jamie's gaze was fixed on the shirt on the table. "No," She says slowly "I missed her greatly during our time apart but if I had pressed on, she might never have appeared at my door that day." She takes a moment to gather her composure before standing. "I might have a box of pictures of Lily and baby Charlie from your guys' playdates. If I find them, I'll give them to you for her." She kissed his head and walked to the door.

Oliver nodded and stood up, going over to the table to pack up the shirt.

"Oliver one thing I learned in life is that waiting for the perfect moment often means missing out entirely," Jamie says softly before walking out.

Oliver's eyes lingered on the shirt for a moment. He nodded slightly, his lips pressing together in a contemplative line. He picked up the shirt and left.

Chapter 10

Pressed Flowers & Gold Jewelry

Charlie had the house to herself. Skylar was running errands; Aaron was working, and Victor was at his friend's house. Amelie had been spending time with her mother since she had the day off work. It's anyone's guess as to where Oliver was.

During moments when she had time alone, she liked to look through the box of mementos she had of her mother. Things Lily left for her, her things that were given from Aaron or Vivian. The box she was planning to look through was a warm, mellowed reddish-brown hue mahogany box. The wood had a distinctive worn look due to years of use and care. Her hands ran over the smooth surface of the top of the box before lifting the lid. Inside were all sorts of different mementos, letters, pictures, souvenirs, poems, and gold jewelry. There were so many contents in the box that the frayed interior lining could barely be seen.

Charlie had left Vivian's house with this precious item back when she was told about her mother's old boyfriend, Grayson. It was filled with things given to Lily by Grayson, items from their dates, and even things Lily collected that reminded her of him.

She moved to the center of her room and laid on her stomach to look through the contents. She carefully took out the small pieces of gold jewelry and set them next to the box. She noticed that there were more rings and necklaces than there were earrings or bracelets.

Next, she pulled out a few smaller items. Movie and concert tickets, a flower key chain, a napkin with lyrics written and a small doodle of a garden on it, a coaster from an old restaurant, and a frame with pressed flowers. Charlie admired the flowers, even though their color faded slightly, they were still preserved in a nice arrangement. There were lilies and what were assumed through little research were primroses. Charlie assumed that Grayson had given Lily these flowers, the lilies representing her, but there wasn't a clear answer about the primroses, they could have just been her favorite flower.

With all the items saved from their dates, it was obvious that even though Grayson came from money it wasn't something he flaunted. The coaster had been from a small diner that Charlie remembers her mom taking her to when she was younger. It had looked a little run down inside, but the staff was nice, and the food tasted amazing. She stopped going there because it reminded her of her mom.

The flower key chain came from the convenience shop she had always gone to when school ended with Amelia and Oliver for an after-school snack. There was a rack of similar-styled key chains by the door.

Her mother was never one for big showy gifts, so it made sense that the most expensive things in here were concert tickets and jewelry. Grayson really loved Lily the way she was meant to be loved.

Before Charlie could go through any more of the box her phone rang. A picture of Oliver standing in a cardboard cutout of a mermaid lit up on the screen. She answered and put him on speaker "Yes Ollie?"

"Can I come over?"

"Yeah"

"Great, cause I'm outside."

He hung up and she let out a small laugh. She didn't mind looking through her mother's things with either of her friends. They were respectful and didn't mind when Lily was mentioned.

"I come bearing gifts," Oliver said walking into the room holding up a light blue shirt.

Charlie read the quote, remembering she was the one to say it but not remembering when.

"What do we got going on here" He set the sweatshirt on a chair before he walked over to sit next to her, making sure he didn't step on anything that surrounded the box.

"I'm just looking through this box Vivian gave me. It's filled with stuff from my mom's first boyfriend." She picked up the framed pressed flowers and admired them.

"Oh cool. Lillies and Primroses, you know what they say about primroses?" He didn't really wait for her to answer. "They represent eternal love."

Lillies and a flower that represents eternal love.

"Who is this mysterious guy?" Oliver reached over and picked up a photo.

Charlie looked over to see a photo of a man. He was tall with an athletic build. He had high cheekbones, and a strong jawline, his deep brown hair contrasted well with his fair complexion. His hair was styled neatly, he wore a crisp dress shirt and black pants with dress shoes. He was leaning against a wall, smiling at the person behind the camera. Although he was leaning, his posture was more upright and confident, like he belonged wherever he was. Charlie remembered Vivian saying he carried himself with authority and composure, that he had a sense of control and leadership, yet still seemed approachable. It was something her mom fell for, something that was evident even in this picture.

"That's Grayson," she said softly. "It's a good picture of him but my favorite one is this one," she said looking through the box.

"How come I've never seen this stuff before?" he asked softly.

Charlie shrugs "I don't look at it often, it feels like it shouldn't be messed with" Charlie had been thinking about love, about how her mother had been loved. It reminded her of the box Vivian had given her, and now where she was.

"He looks stylish" Oliver ran his fingers through his hair, "I bet I could style my hair like that."

Oliver had dark brown hair which was usually styled messily but it suited him. "You have too many layers, Grayson's is slicked back and sometimes has a side part. You don't part your hair."

"Yeah, I don't want to mess with my perfectly tousled look. It takes forever to get it just right" He teased.

Charlie finally pulled out her favorite picture. It was a close-up of her mom and Grayson's faces. It was cut off just above their chins, their eyes were wide, and they both were smiling big. Grayson had light blue, almost icy eyes. Charlie found that they were a poetic comparison to her mother's amber-brown eyes. She thought it was cute that his eyes seemed icy and hers were warm. The photo was angled just right so that it hit her eyes giving them a soft sunlight glow.

"They look happy," Oliver noted. "And all this stuff is from Grayson? What's in the letters?"

The only thing left in the box were letters stuffed in envelopes and scraps of loose paper with poems and love notes written on them. "I don't know, I haven't read them." She looked up and met his quizzical look. "I just feel like they aren't mine to read, opening an envelope feels wrong. Although, I did read some of the poems and notes he wrote her" She took out a few pieces of paper and handed him some.

"To have been regarded like nature" Oliver read "That is how she sees me, poetic when I fear I am nothing more than ordinary."

Charlie picked up another piece and read it aloud "Picture, a house where it doesn't matter where things go, as long as they are next to each other. It's warm, that is how I'll live with you."

"This must be what it is like to be loved enough to the point of creation" Oliver spoke softly, his eyes trailing over the items on the floor. "When you're loved by an artist you are brought along in all of their pieces."

Charlie looked down at the picture of her mom and Grayson, she couldn't stop herself from looking over to the light blue sweatshirt resting on her chair.

Oliver and Charlie spent a little over an hour going through the box of her mom's things. She told him stories about her mom that were passed from Vivian, he listened and would ask questions.

Now they were walking to the park after treating themselves to ice cream. Charlie got a cup of sherbert, and Oliver got a cone with one scoop of chocolate. "You know you could do more than work at a library," Oliver said suddenly.

Charlie was kind of surprised that he had brought up the earlier topic of her job choice. She didn't say anything, just kept her eyes down at her sherbert.

"Now, I'm not saying you shouldn't or that it's a bad idea, but Amelie is right. You could do so much more if you wanted it," he shrugs "I think she's going about it in her own way. I don't think you wanting to stay here is what is keeping you cursed."

Charlie's head snapped up and she looked over at him. "You don't?"

Oliver met her eyes and gave her a small smile "No Char, I'm staying here for college too."

"But you didn't get cursed" Charlie pointed out.

"I know, I don't think you wanting to go to college here and work here is the reason. Trying to motivate you to find another job probably isn't the solution."

"What is?"

Oliver shrugged and licked the cone where some ice cream had melted. "I dunno, but even when Amelie graduates just know it won't be the end. I'll still be here to help."

Charlie would be lying if she said the thought of Oliver leaving didn't crush her as much as Amelie having to leave. Typically, Charlie found that in friend groups, there were two friends that were way closer than anyone else. That wasn't the case in Charlie's mind, she loved both of her friends equally and neither one of them got more of her time than the other.

The two made their way over to a park bench. Charlie sat down after doing a quick seat check for any bugs. She took a bite of her ice cream and looked around. Her thoughts were running through her head begging to spill out. Most times, Charlie didn't like to talk about what was going on in her head, but most times she had too much going on that she felt like she was going to burst.

She turned back to Oliver who finished off the last of his cone and had his eyes trained on a dog that was being walked across the street from them. "Hey Ollie" she started for a moment but stopped.

Oliver looked at her and met her eyes. "Yeah, Char?"

Charlie hated eye contact, she felt like she looked ridiculous, like she was staring too long. But right now, she studied the color of his eyes and mentally prepared herself. "I miss Vivian you know," she says after a moment.

Oliver didn't look surprised; he didn't have much of a facial expression. He was good at that, Charlie thought. He always had a way of making a person feel heard with no judgment.

"I know." He said.

Charlie put the spoon in her mouth and chewed on the plastic for a moment before taking it out, putting it in her cup, and speaking again. "Ms. Vivian was the closest I felt to my mom. I mean I know I'm living with my uncle but he's always working and when he's not…" She shrugs "I can't bring myself to talk about her." She waited for Oliver to say something, a quick response. An 'I get what you mean' or something. But he didn't

So, she continued.

"Vivian knew my mom; she would go to her house all the time. It was like Ms. V knew everything about her" Her expression grows somber, lost in thought. "It was hard enough losing mom. I mean I don't even really remember what happened. I was twelve, and I was staying the night at Aaron's. Mom was supposed to... she had something going on" She played the memory in her head again. It was late and she had been woken up by Aaron's voice from downstairs. He was on the phone with someone, talking about her mother and her whereabouts.

Young Charlie had crept out of the guest room and watched from the top of the stairs, in time to see Aaron hang up the phone, kiss Skylar's head, and rush out the door. She remembered not knowing what was going on, so she went back to bed. She woke up a few hours later to the sounds of different voices, and when she went to the top of the stairs, she saw police officers, Aaron, Skylar, and Ms. Vivian. Charlie went downstairs and hugged Vivian's arm, not sure what was happening.

She met Aaron's eyes, and he hung his head and went to the kitchen, being followed by Skylar. Charlie remembered the way the tears stained his face.

Vivian had guided her outside away from the commotion and broke the news gently. Well as gently as one could tell a 12-year-old that their mother passed away in a car accident.

Charlie's mind was still spiraling with this flashback when she felt a warm hand on hers. She blinked a few times, looked at Oliver's hand, and then back up at him. He gave her a comforting look and a small nod. Charlie looked up at the sky and took a deep breath trying to keep her voice still.

"But Ms. Vivian was always there for me, and I hate that she left. I hate that she only left me with that acorn key chain. I mean what does it even mean!" she exclaimed, her hands moving up to her head. Her elbows rested on the table, head in her hands, a little regretful that she pulled away from Oliver's warm touch. "I hate that Amelie is leaving, and I hate how upset that makes me" she admits. "I didn't express that before, and I know it makes her sad when I do that."

"Did she come and talk to you?" Oliver asked softly.

Charlie nodded, her head not leaving her hands. "Yeah, I know she understands. She came over and we talked about it all." She paused and moved her hands. "But I am no closer to figuring out what will keep me from being stuck here."

She let out a short laugh and shook her head. "I just feel really lost."

Oliver's eyes trailed over her face. He hated seeing her so upset, hated that he couldn't fix it for her.

"Do you want to hear more about your mom?"

Chapter 11

Moments with Ms. Vivian

"Ms. Vivian." Charlie was helping her reorganize her bookshelf that day. She had gotten a bigger bookshelf and wanted to get rid of the smaller one. "I've been thinking about my dad."

"Oh?" she said softly.

"There aren't any pictures of him. Aaron has all the photo albums from my grandparent's house and the ones from my mom. There's none of my dad."

Vivian didn't say anything. She had mastered the art of not speaking until the other person had emptied all the thoughts from their head.

Charlie hesitated knowing once the question was out there, she was going to get an answer. Even if she didn't like it. "Was my dad a bad person?"

"Your father met your mom a few years after your mom started working at the family business full time. He came in and charmed your mother, enough for her to come back and tell me about it." She chuckled softly "She wasn't won over so easily; I don't think she was open to anyone else coming in since she lost contact with Grayson. But after a few months of your father coming in and asking your mother out. She agreed"

Charlie's nose scrunched up and her lips pursed together. "He wore her down? That's not very romantic." Charlie didn't know much about her father, except that his name was Christopher. She had hoped that however her dad met her mom it would at least be romantic.

Vivian chuckled softly "That's what I thought, but I held my tongue because it wasn't my story to write."

"Okay, so he came into the store a lot, wore her down. Did they go on a date? Was it a good one?"

Vivian nodded. "They went on a date to the Diner. She learned that he was a bank teller, but he wanted to travel the world," She thought for a moment "Your mother wanted to travel as well so I think that gained a bit of her interest."

Her head tilted as she waited for more, but Vivian's storytelling seemed to fall short when it came to talking about Christopher. "So did you meet him too?"

The older woman huffed like it had been a silly question "Of course I did, child."

"And?"

"And there was nothing memorable about him."

Charlie squeezed her eyes shut and took a breath. She had no feelings towards Vivian calling her father boring, she didn't even know him enough to take offense to that. But Vivian was the only one who would talk about Christopher, and they were getting nowhere.

"Please Ms. Vivian" her voice was so quiet she could barely hear it herself. "I need to know."

"You knowing someone else's past will not help you build your future," she says after a moment.

She opened her eyes and looked at her confused. "What?"

"You want to know about your father in hopes you'll figure yourself out and I'm afraid you will not get the answers you want."

"This isn't about that. I want to know about this guy who was remarkable enough to be my father but not enough to have pictures of in photo albums. There isn't even any trace of him giving my mother gifts like Grayson had. I want to know why."

"He did give her gifts." Came her simple reply.

"What do you mean?"

Vivian paused a moment, taking her time to stack her pile of books organized by color. "When I first met Christopher, he wasted no time telling me about himself. He had big plans but talked about them in an unachievable way. He had plans for your mother and they had only been together a week." She moved the books with orange on them over to Charlie to put away and started collecting books with purple in them. "He gifted your mother silver jewelry during the first few weeks."

Charlie knew that her mother disliked silver jewelry, claiming that felt that gold made her feel beautiful. Young Charlie had only ever seen her mom in gold, only ever seen gold pieces in her childhood bedroom, only ever seen it in the mahogany box that now resided under her bed. Even the ring she wore on her right ring finger was gold, her mom had said it was her favorite piece of jewelry, so it belonged to her favorite person.

"Your mother started to spend a lot of time with Christopher, I had started to see her less. Then after her parents passed, she came to me. It was the night after the funeral, I had asked where Christopher was. She told me he was out with friends;

he didn't attend the funeral with her. She said that he had talked about her moving in with him. He had plans to travel then settle and start a family."

"But mom was supposed to keep the family business going?"

Vivian nodded. "She wanted to stay here more than ever but Christopher never wanted to be stuck here." She pushed the books down the line and started with a different color. "I told her that if running the business wasn't what she wanted to do then don't do it but use that time to pursue her real dream." She looked over. "Do you remember what your mother had a passion for?"

Charlie was young when her mom passed away, and to younger Charlie, Lily was talented with everything. There wasn't any one thing that stuck out that might be her mother's dream. Charlie shook her head after not coming up with an answer.

"She wanted to be a singer."

Charlie thought back to being young when her mom was always singing. She sang in the car, in the kitchen, she sang her to sleep. She had a song for every occasion good and bad. "She was a good singer."

Vivian nodded softly. "She was. She sang for every school choir and talent show, at church, she even performed a few times at the Diner on third street," She says then laughs slightly "There was never a karaoke event your mom didn't attend."

A warm smile spread across Charlie's face listening to the stories of her mom. She enjoyed hearing about her mom's passion for singing. It made her feel closer to her mother.

"She even got accepted to Julliard."

This was new information to Charlie. "Mom never told me about this." She always heard that she stayed and worked at the store with Aaron.

"I was the first one she told." she said softly. "She got a letter. She got accepted and she was excited to go and have a chance to do something she was passionate about."

"Why didn't she go?" she asked quietly, afraid of the answer.

"Well, she told Christopher. But he already had his own plans." She stared down at the pile of books in front of her, to anyone else it would seem that she was looking for any more books with the same color, but Charlie could tell she was reliving that moment.

"He didn't let her go to the school?" Charlie asked quietly. "He wanted to move away right, but Mom never moved away."

"He didn't let her go to the school. He convinced her that she could do so much more by being his wife, by staying home and providing for them. It wasn't any different than what she had done when her parents had gotten older, he had told her." Vivian shook her head slightly "So they came to a compromise of sorts. She agreed to stay here with him and not go to school, and he decided he could live here with her. They bought the house you grew up and your mother divided her time between being a homemaker and helping her brother."

"She didn't get to live her dream."

"She was too busy living everyone else's," Vivian concluded.

The thought of her mother not being able to go to school to sing broke Charlie's heart. She couldn't bear to think of Lily being convinced to stay here and cook and clean for Christopher when she had her own dreams and aspirations.

"They got married after five months of being together. He stopped buying her jewelry and started buying her aprons, and cookware. All her awards, stage costumes, and performance videos were packed in boxes and left in my house. Which I gave to Aaron soon after her passing."

"My mom was miserable," Charlie said quietly, piecing together why there had been no pictures of Christopher. He changed the path of her life.

"Oh, but she found out she was pregnant with you," Vivian said looking up, a soft expression on her face. "She was excited, overjoyed. When you were born, you were like her mini-me. Oh, she adored you, Charlie!" She spoke. "Lily brought you over every chance she got. I remember being in the kitchen putting snacks together for her before she had to go to work. She was singing you to sleep. It was the first time I heard her sing in a long time."

Charlie smiled softly at the mention of her mother being overjoyed at her arrival, but she decided she wouldn't ask much about her father anymore after that.

Chapter 12

Grayson Kingsley

"Here it is" Jamie walked into the kitchen with a box that she sat down in front of Oliver and Charlie.

Oliver had told Charlie that his mother knew her mother in college, and they spent some time again when the two were younger, way before they reunited again in fifth grade. Charlie was a bit surprised about this, she didn't know her mother and Jamie knew each other in college. She just assumed they had become friends because of the kids.

But now, sitting at the Knight's kitchen table looking through the box, she saw more into her mother's past. She often forgot that her mother had a life before having a kid, that Lily May was a child, a teen, a young adult. Her own person.

"Oh, there are so many things inside this box," Jamie tells Charlie, settling in the chair next to Oliver who had sat to Charlie's left. "A few college photos and then a majority of the pictures in there are of us when you two were younger."

Charlie picked up a picture of her mother holding a small baby wrapped in a white blanket. Lily had sat on the floor of the Knight's living room. She wasn't looking at the camera, instead her gaze was down at a small bundle of blanket, there was a soft glow of love on her face. Lily's hair was a magnificent halo of tightly coiled curls, framing her face.

Charlie instinctively moved her hand to her hair. Seeing how her hair resembled her mother's made her feel closer to her, made her feel even more beautiful.

"Your mother came to me one day a little frantic" Jamie chuckled softly "You wouldn't stop crying and she was worried she was doing something wrong, something all mothers go through at some point."

Charlie's eyes stayed glued to the picture, taking in everything about her mother's presence in this photo. It made sense for Jamie to be a guiding light for a new mother. At the time, she had three sons, and Oliver was her middle kid, so Jamie had had some knowledge by the time Lily had come around with Charlie.

"She kind of had to do it alone," Charlie said reaching for another picture. This picture was of Lily sitting on the floor with baby Charlie. Charlie was sitting on the floor in front of her mother leaning against her, a block held tightly in her hand. Jamie was sitting next to Lily, they were in conversation, and a baby Oliver was on his hands and knees reaching for the block that Charlie had.

"Kind of," Jamie hummed "She had Aaron, Vivian, me, and Angela" She nodded softly "Of course around that time Aaron didn't have kids, and Vivian only could do so much. Angela was still a new mom as well." She carefully picked up the picture "I promised her that she was doing a great job. She was. Your mother was fantastic, sometimes I don't know how she did it. Running that family business and looking after you."

Charlie put the photo down and picked up a few other ones. These did not have Charlie in them but showcased college years. There was a picture of her mother, Jamie, and another girl smiling. They seemed to be in one of their dorm rooms. She flipped over the picture and read the words scrawled on the back

"Sleepover. We almost got people in our hall kicked out."

She put that picture down and picked up another picture. This was a photo that captured her mother and Jamie head-on. The two sat in a classroom, easels and paint in front of them. *"Art Class"* was written on the back.

Charlie picked up one more picture and this one made her breath catch in her throat. This picture was taken at Charlie's home. Lily was not the focus in this picture. She sat next to a man and seemed to be admiring the view that was taking place beside her. Grayson sat on the floor holding that familiar bundle of blankets gently in his arms.

"Oh," Jamie said with a softness in her voice. "That's Grayson. He always supported your mother. Even when you were born, he came by a few times to help look after you. I don't know why he stopped visiting afterward, but I know he sent your mother money."

Charlie's eyes were glued to the picture. Grayson had seen her when she was a baby, he was still present even after he had moved away. Why was it that Grayson was more present than her own father? She needed to know when Grayson had fully cut off contact with her mother.

"When was the last time you saw him? Grayson? With my mom?" Charlie spoke slowly almost like she was scared of the answer. Maybe because she was.

"Oh uhm," Jamie thought for a moment "I know he would babysit when your mom had work. I think that last time he had been around you were two years old?"

"Where was Christopher?"

Jamie raised her eyebrow feeling like this was entering territory she wasn't supposed to be. "I know he worked a lot or was out of town a lot. Your mom didn't talk much about him."

Charlie thought for a moment, it was possible that Grayson came back for her mother but due to her fears of Christopher she didn't leave with him. Jamie said the last time she had seen Grayson was when Charlie was two. If the two were still close, then Grayson would have heard about Lily's parents' passing, and he would've come to visit. "Did he come to the funeral?"

Jamie thought for a moment and then shook her head. "It was a while ago, but I don't think he was there."

"Neither was Christopher" Charlie mumbled to herself. "Thanks for this Jamie, I really do appreciate it. More than you know" she got out of her chair "Thank you!" She booked it out of the house. Filled with confidence to ask Aaron about her mother.

Chapter 13

A Funeral Invite & A Journal

Charlie had been pacing around in her room, walking too fast for her feet to fully sink into the cushy carpet. She knew Aaron would be home soon, he had only worked a half day today, which gave Charlie the opportunity to work up the courage to ask about her mom. She needed to go in there with a plan, and she needed to catch Aaron at the right time. She didn't want to bombard him with questions that would stir up painful memories, especially not if he had had an exhausting day.

The girl stopped walking for a moment, taking a deep breath, she let herself stand completely still. She let her feet sink into the carpet, taking a moment to feel the soft texture under her bare feet. It was the only time she allowed herself to walk barefoot, she hated the feeling of the hardwood floor that occupied most of the house. She twisted the ring on her finger and figured out exactly what she wanted to ask Aaron.

What did she want to know about her mom that she hadn't already learned? What were his thoughts on Grayson? Did he know he was helping Mom when she was a baby?

Why her thoughts went directly to Grayson, she wasn't sure. She knew her mother was more than her partners. She knew that Christopher had tried to change her. Mom wanted to be something great, but stayed here for Christopher, stayed here for her parents.

Mom was going to go to school for music. Did she want to be a singer? Did she ever perform for her family? What was it that Mom had wanted to do when she was younger? What did she go to college for?

Charlie had a good glimpse of her mother's personality from stories from Ms. Vivian and Jamie. She wanted to know about her mother's dreams. It made her sad that she had given them up. However, she made a promise to herself to not bring up Christopher to Aaron, nor would she bring up the fact that Mom never left Grand Fayword.

The heavy, front door downstairs closed shut and she heard Aaron's voice on the phone. This was it; the time was now. She looked down at her finger to make sure her ring was still on her finger, a nervous habit that resulted in her fearing she would lose it, and then made her way downstairs. She found Aaron in the living room, still on the phone.

He noticed her, smiled, and shortly ended the call "Hey Lee, how is your day going?"

"It's good," she said with a small nod. "Uhm, I was wondering if I could talk to you about something?"

Aaron's eyebrows knitted together, and he frowned slightly. "Is everything alright?"

Charlie nodded quickly not wanting to worry him "Yes! I uhm. I just wanted to... ask you questions about Mom."

Aaron's shoulders sank a little, but it was noticeable to Charlie. "Well, I guess you are old enough to understand without me having to beat around the bush," he sat down on the couch, and patted the seat next to him "What is it that you want to know?"

The first part was done. Now came the hardest, the conversation. Charlie sat down next to him and looked down at her hands, not daring to make eye contact yet. "What did mom want to be when she was younger?"

Charlie didn't have to look at his face to know that that question had thrown him off "Oh…" He was quiet for a moment "I'm not really sure, I guess I never really asked her. She had a lot of hobbies though."

"Like what?"

"Singing. She loved to do that. She liked dancing and painting; she always gave our grandparents a painting for Christmas" he thought for a moment "Oh she volunteered at the animal shelter quite often."

"What did she go to college for?" She hoped that this would give her some insight into what her mother had wanted to do with her life.

"Business." His answer was short and clear. "We were going to take over our parent's store, you know."

She nodded slowly. Her mother had known she was going to take over the store long enough for her to go to college for business. Why did it pain her to hear those words? "Did. Did Mom want to help?"

The man sighed, sounding a little worn out "Your mother didn't necessarily want to help. But she knew it was the right thing to do."

"She wanted to go to Julliard. For singing, didn't she?" She looked up and met his eyes, a confused expression on his face "Ms. Vivian told me a little about it."

"Of course she did" he muttered before straightening up "Yes, Lily told me she had gotten into Julliard. She was excited about it, but I didn't hear much about it after that"

"That's because your sister was indecisive and a bit of a scatterbrain" A new voice had spoken up. Standing atop the stairs stood Skylar. "Sorry love, I don't mean to speak ill of the dead but even you were worried about what she was going to do with her life."

Charlie did not like how Skylar was talking about her mom. This was the first negative thing she had heard about her mother and of course, it had to come from Skylar.

"Yes, Lily was a bit hesitant with her choices, but she meant well. She was a smart girl" Aaron said turning to his wife.

"I was worried about her for a moment. Then she got married and I figured everything would work out for her" Skylar made her way down the stairs. The elegant way she held herself and walked did not match the condescension that dripped from her words.

"What is that supposed to mean?" Charlie snapped.

The blonde woman looked surprised but fixed her expression, giving a small shrug "Well I figured it would be easier for her to be more stable with her decisions if she had someone else helping her" She sat on a chair and crossed her legs. "She did better when her parents and Aaron told her to go to school to help with the business, she seemed more responsible with someone's… guidance."

"Skylar," Aaron's voice was dejected, and he ran his hand down his face "Don't do this right now."

"What?" Skylar pouts "All I'm saying is that Lily would have never got it figured out if Christopher-"

"Skylar!" Aaron shouted. "Stop with his name and stop talking about them" he stood up "I can't with this conversation anymore." He looked at Charlie and sighed "I'm sorry Lee" He walked upstairs.

"You want to know something?" Skylar asked the second he was out of earshot.

Charlie's eyes followed him until he disappeared. She wasn't sure she had the energy to hear any more from Skylar.

Of course, she spoke anyway. "Christopher is the reason Lily's high school sweetheart never made it to her parent's funeral."

"What?" She gave her the attention that she so desperately craved, but she didn't care. This was one of the things she had been wondering.

"I might've gotten a little bored one night when Aaron and I had come over to have dinner with Lily and Christopher" She started speaking slowly, knowing how much Charlie had wanted to hear this. "I might've taken myself on a little walk around the house and seen Christopher coming out of the bathroom looking as guilty as a dog… So, I wandered myself in there and found an envelope in the trash. It had 'Grayson Kingsley' written on it and inside was a letter telling him that Loretta and Stephen May had died, it was asking for his attendance at their funeral. It was signed by Lily."

"Why didn't you tell mom? Or even Aaron?"

"I didn't tell Aaron because I didn't want to add more stress on him. He probably would've just gotten angry and fought Christopher. I wasn't really in the mood to watch a fight" she said casually.

"Why didn't you tell my mother" Charlie reiterated.

"Oh" Skylar sounded shocked, as if it was a completely new concept "I guess I didn't think about that" She stood up "It was great to catch up, but maybe don't bother your uncle with this anymore, okay? He has enough to worry about." She started up the stairs "Oh and Charlie. You do plan on living elsewhere when you graduate right?"

It was getting late, Charlie had eaten dinner with the family, and it had felt awkward in her mind. Luckily Victor hadn't gotten the memo because he had rambled on about the Nerf gun war he had with his friend Lukas.

Now Charlie was lying in bed, not ready to sleep in the slightest. She hadn't brushed her teeth or washed her face; she wasn't even dressed for it yet. Her mind was replaying the conversation she had with Aaron and the irritating one with Skylar. She had learned nothing more about her mother, nothing that had helped her. All she learned was Christopher sucked, but she already knew that.

There was a soft knock on her door, followed by it opening slowly "Hey Lce," Aaron walked into her room slowly, with a notebook in his hand. "I'm sorry about how that conversation went. I'm sorry about Skylar and how I didn't answer any of your questions."

Charlie sat up and gave a small shrug "It was a long shot. I knew it would be hard for you to talk about her. It's okay."

He sighed softly "I got to be honest kid, I wasn't prepared for those questions, I didn't really know Lily like that," He chuckled softly "It sounds stupid to say that I didn't even know the one I grew up with, but it's true. I only really knew her on the surface." He started "I knew what everyone already did, I knew about her hobbies because she made damn sure I was involved." He laughed a bit thinking back to some memories "Every talent show, every dance recital. I was there for it all. I met Grayson. I liked him. Wish he had stuck around. Wish Christopher hadn't."

Charlie wanted to press on but decided to learn from Oliver and stay silent to see what else Aaron would reveal.

"But I didn't ever really talk to her about what she wanted to do. We never talked about life or our feelings or anything like that. We both agreed to go to school to learn how to take over the business for our parents." He paused, and his eyes closed "It killed me a bit inside when I reminded Lily that she couldn't leave with Grayson. I got mad at her for not wanting to stay when I was going to. A little mad that my parents were easier on her for not wanting to stick around when they inevitably passed." His voice caught in his throat "I felt like a villain when she cried over Grayson leaving. She was distant after that, she just worked, and we talked about business. It felt the same but… different in a way."

Aaron opened his eyes and shifted his weight. "I often wonder what would've happened if I convinced her to go with Grayson." he looks down at Charlie "But I don't think too hard about it because then I wouldn't have you" He smiled "You look a lot like her. She loved you like mad."

Charlie smiled a bit at the reassurance that Aaron did love her and wanted her around. She would never tire of hearing how she looked like her mother. That her mother had loved her.

"I think she would want you to have this." He hands her the small book he had come in with.

Charlie took it and looked at the cover. It was a worn green hard-cover journal with faded printed flowers on it. It was secured closed with a green elastic band stretched around the cover.

"I can't answer your questions, but who better to answer questions about Lily than Lily herself?"

Charlie looked up and gave him a soft smile "Thank you so much."

In her hands, she held the secrets of her mother. She was going to learn who she was, and what she wanted to do. How she planned to spend her life.

She was finally going to make sense of her own life.

Chapter 14

Lily's Journal

I have no idea what the hell I am doing.

Chapter 15

Lily's Journal Page 2

I remember being younger and always having a new idea for what I wanted to do when I got older. I wanted to be an astronaut, a horse trainer, a doctor, a lawyer, a teacher, a writer. I figured around middle school that the best approach to eventually figuring out what I wanted to do was to be the best at everything.

So, I did.

I tried out for volleyball, soccer, and basketball for school. (I only ever liked volleyball) I begged Mom to let me do gymnastics, which I thoroughly enjoyed and excelled at until Aaron scared me during practice, and I fell on the balance beam (Thanks…) I joined academy dance and moved up into competitive dance.

In school, I took a lot of business classes, art classes, and language classes. In my free time, I perfected those art and language skills. I joined the debate club and ran for class president (I lost by one vote. I suspect Aaron as he had a crush on my opponent Katherine Langley).

Voice lessons were definitely my favorite.

I did everything and still maintained perfect grades and social friend groups. I was always busy and basked in the praise I got from others who were amazed at how much I could do. How I was staying out of trouble, how I would have no trouble exceeding in the real world with "talent like that"

I didn't realize the burnout I was feeling.

I didn't realize it until I met Grayson. (Good job Sophomore me). He came to all my events and was always the loudest one to cheer me on.

He seemed to have it all figured out. He also joined the debate club, he was well-spoken, charming, and dressed sharply. He said he was going to take over his father's business.

I told him he was lucky to have a plan.

He told me he didn't want to follow in his father's footsteps. He ran a winery that Gray had deemed pointless. He told me he wanted to help people. Make a difference for others.

He told me about how his father ditched him and his mother. How Grayson had to step up and help. He said he never wanted anyone to struggle. Yes, his mother had money, but money didn't matter when she had no motivation to "start over"

Grayson wanted to help others like he helped his mother.

Aaron has been telling me we should think about helping with the family business. I am a Senior in high school. I think I have to make a choice.

I love my parents, but I never really thought about running the store, not deeply. It was always something I was told "would be mine one day" but I never really thought about what that would entail.

Lily's Journal Page 3

I like singing.

I love it actually. I think it might be the one thing I've stuck with so far. I've dropped all my sports since starting Senior year. I don't have as many classes this year either. I've spent most of my time working part-time at the store, at voice lessons, hanging out with Ms. Vivian, and spending time with Grayson.

I enjoy spending time with him. I feel a lot lighter around him, I have less time to worry about what I'm going to do with my life. I don't feel the pressure to be great all the time. I just exist.

Grayson wants to take me on expensive dates, nice dinners, and shopping trips in the city. He'd spend however much I asked just to make me happy.

I don't want that. I make him take me to Sun Set Grove for the millionth. They have amazing pasta. I make sure to bring my camera so I can fill up my room with pictures of us.

He has a picture of me in his wallet, I don't know when he took it. I'm sitting in his living room on the couch. I know I was looking out the window, most likely looking at a dog judging by my excitement.

I thought I looked like a nut.

He said I looked beautiful.

It's a nice picture. It's nice to see myself from a different perspective.

I guess I don't really know myself from my own perspective.

I want to.

Anytime anyone asks me what I want to do when I get older, I can see the disappointment and feel the awkwardness when I tell them I want to go into the arts. But when I tell them I want to go into business (Maybe I do?) They seem to light up and rant and rave about how great of an idea that is. So that's what I must do.

Lily's Journal Page 4

I got a letter from Julliard. I sent in an audition as a joke. Well, I guess it wasn't really a joke, I referred to it as a joke as protection in case I got rejected.

Grayson and I talked one night about graduation. We graduate soon, I don't know what I want to do. Maybe I won't find it here. Grayson has to leave after college. I could follow him.

I'm not stupid, I wouldn't just follow him if he didn't want it, I wouldn't plan my whole life over some guy (God I would rather die than be controlled the rest of my life by a man) Grayson isn't like that though.

I wonder if I can find my meaning out there, outside of Grand Fayword.

Oh wait, I forgot I was writing about Julliard. Anyway, yes, I got scared about graduating high school without a real plan. Grayson had asked me what it was that made me feel something deeply in my bones.

I was honest, I told him I didn't know. That I had tried everything under the sun to try and figure myself out. There was only one thing that stuck with me but that wasn't a career.

He told me it was a driving force. That our careers don't have to be our passion. As long as we have something in our lives that makes us feel motivated. That was all we needed.

I sent in a tape.

I got accepted.

I told Grayson and Ms. Vivian

I was going to perform. I always wanted to perform.

I want to go to Juilliard. I do not want to stay here forever and work at my parent's store. I love them, I love them, I do. But the store is their driving force. Not mine.

Lily's Journal Page 5

Dear Past Lily

We messed up. But that's fine. I never told my parents about Julliard. Aaron told me I should go to school for business to help him when it is our time to take over the store. Business classes aren't bad, I made a friend, Jamie Evergreen.

I made a lot of friends here. I know I don't write a lot here, but I've taken pictures, I'm experiencing these moments. Who would want to read my experiences? They wouldn't mean anything to anyone else but me.

I still have doubts about running the store. I think about trying again for Julliard after college. I got a full ride, they want me. I try not to think too much about it. I spend my time with Grayson and Jamie.

I put on vocal performances at diners, I do them cause Jamie dares me, but I have fun, and no one has told me that I bother them, so I keep going.

I don't want to think about how Grayson will be leaving after we graduate. We are only freshmen, but I can't stop thinking about it. I would want to go with him.

I don't have anything pictured for my life. I enjoy what's happening now, I enjoy these moments because I know I will never get them back. The only constant I see when I try and imagine my life (before having to stop so I don't send myself down a panic spiral) is

Grayson. I imagine coming home and making dinner with him. Doing menial household chores. I feel content knowing that there is a possibility that I come home to Grayson every day.

Lily's Journal Page 6

I know. I don't write. Does it even matter? I have already experienced these moments. Why would I want to relive them? Why would I want to show them to anyone else?

Grayson is gone. We graduated. He had to go take over his father's business in order to get money. He said he wanted to be able to provide as best as he could for me.

I told him I didn't care about him.

I cried to Ms. Vivian when he left. I cried in front of Aaron.

I stayed in town and worked with Aaron at the store. I don't think about Julliard. I don't sing anymore. I don't know what Jamie is up to these days.

I don't tell anyone that Grayson promised me he would come back with enough money to give to my parents' store so that I don't have to work here anymore.

I don't tell anyone I feel a little resentment to this store.

I barely used this page, so I guess I'll fill it up. I met a guy named Christopher. He is not as nice as Grayson, but no one is. I've lost contact with Grayson. I hope he's doing well.

Christopher doesn't like that I work at the store. He says he wants to get married. I know what he wants. He wants me to do what I have done for everyone else my whole life, whatever he wants.

Julliard is out of the picture. I've been given silver jewelry and cookware.

Before I knew it, I was living with Christopher. I've kept all my stuff safe at Ms. Vivian's after he threw it up in the attic. All my stage attire, awards, and performance books. Everything that I am, he locked away.

I work at the store and then come home and cook and clean.

I think about Grayson.

I feel content knowing that there is another reality that I would come home to Grayson every day.

I never wanted mediocre love, I wanted someone to build me a stage.

Chapter 16

Volleyball Therapy Session

"Mine!" Amelie screams before diving to the ground, making contact with both the grassy surface and the leather of the volleyball. The ball sailed over the net and right past Oliver's raised hands.

The group was at the park playing volleyball. Well, Oliver and Amelie had decided to play the game, Charlie, however, was sitting on top of a picnic table just watching the game. This was not unusual, the two didn't leave Charlie out, nor did she feel excluded. She often preferred to sit back and watch instead of participating. She claimed she had more fun that way.

"Tell me why you quit volleyball again?" Oliver asked while jogging over to pick up the volleyball that had rolled a few feet behind him.

"I had other things I needed to worry about," Amelie said, shrugging slightly. "I mean yeah leaving before my Senior year really sucks but, I wanted to focus more on classes and applying to colleges."

Oliver just nodded slightly before tossing the ball back over to Amelie so she could serve. "You didn't want to enjoy the last year of volleyball?"

Amelie walked to the corner designated for serving, she stared at him for a moment "I'll miss my teammates but if we're being honest, we are all going to be moving on eventually" She rested the ball in her left palm before throwing it up, her right hand coming down to smack the ball hard over the net. "What's the point of delaying the inevitable?"

Oliver dove for the ball, hitting it hard right back over the net before quickly scrambling up to prepare for her next attack. "It isn't delaying the inevitable, Amelie. It's enjoying every part of what you can before moving on."

"I'm taking the next steps to ensure my future is set" Amelie bumped the ball back over the net. "That is what's important" She watched the ball sail over the net "What are your next plans, Oliver?"

He bumped the ball right back to her, opting for a conversation where they could be fidgeting, instead of a hardcore match. "I'm still on the soccer team, and I plan to keep going through high school" He watched the ball go towards the girl. "I'm staying here for college, wanting to major in graphic design."

Amelie hit the ball back "You're staying here for college? Didn't you get offers for out-of-state schools?"

He glanced over at Charlie who had still just been watching the game. "Yeah?" He took a few steps back to hit the ball back over.

"Well, there are other, better schools that want you, Oliver. Don't you think it's worth giving them a shot?" She backed up, raised her hand, and spiked the ball down.

Oliver braced himself before hitting the ball back over to her. "I want to stay here."

"Why graphic design?"

"It's what I like to do," he tells her.

"I like makeup but I'm not going to school for it." Amelie had been a very talented makeup artist. She was always showing up to school with bold looks. Any event she attended she had elaborate designs for her eyes. Even her birthday makeup was extravagant.

Charlie often envied her for it. She was talented and beautiful enough to pull it off.

"Why don't you?" Oliver asked, "You like doing it, you're crazy good at it."

Amelie rolled her eyes "That wouldn't be a good career. I need to go to a good school and make good money" It was her turn to return the ball, and she spiked the ball towards Oliver. "That's what life is about."

Oliver stepped back and set the ball a few times before hitting it back over to Amelie. "I am taking graphic design because it is something I enjoy. I'm staying with my soccer team because I love being around them. I am staying here for college because there are so many things about this place that I love."

"That is not a very good plan Oliver. Life doesn't work like that, it is important to have a good job, and good connections. Dwelling in your high school years and hometown is not something that can support you in the long run."

"My mom had a fun high school and college experience," Charlie said after a moment. She wasn't looking at anyone in particular, just looking at the swings in the distance. "She wanted to experience life, but Aaron wanted her to find a steady job" She glanced down at the gold ring on her finger "I don't know what life is about, but both my mom and Aaron ended up working at my grandparents' store."

She noticed her friends' silences, so she continued slowly, even though she wasn't sure where she was going with this. "Mom seemed to really thrive in high school and college. She had good friends, was a stellar student. She later got accepted into a music school and found love."

"She found love?" Amelie asked tucking the ball under her arm "Your dad, you mean?"

Charlie met the girl's eyes and shook her head. She had forgotten even to mention finding out about Grayson. "Oh man, I forgot to mention, Ms. Vivian had told me a long time ago about someone my mom dated in high school, Grayson. She had given me a box of stuff my mom kept about him, and I just opened it recently."

Amelie tilted her head "Why did Ms. Vivian have that box?"

Charlie had thought about that too and even though she had never asked the question she assumed it was for the same reason a lot of her mother's prized possessions were at Ms. Vivian's house. Christopher. "They were close" she answered. She had never been brave enough to tell anyone that she knew her father wasn't a great man.

"So, what do we know about this Grayson guy?" she asked, setting the ball on the ground before walking over to sit down on the picnic bench. Oliver followed in suit.

Charlie just shrugged slightly. "I don't know, they dated in high school and all throughout college. They seemed really in love" She kept her spot on top of the table, her eyes not meeting her friends. "They broke up shortly after graduating, Grayson had to move away for a family matter."

Amelie gasps "Oh gosh, what if Grayson is your father!"

Charlie snorted "That's definitely not the case. Skylar has made that abundantly clear."

"What does that mean?" It was Oliver's turn to speak.

"Skylar doesn't like my dad and anytime I did something she didn't like, she compared me to him."

"What is even the point of that?" Amelie scoffs.

"I don't know why she has it out for you Char, you do so much for her," Oliver spoke gently.

Oliver always seemed to speak to her in such a way that made her feel comfortable speaking about things that weighed on her. It made her feel confident that she wasn't annoying anyone and that she was allowed to speak.

Both of her friends played vital parts in getting the girl to speak up. Amelie always showed the right emotion that validated Charlie's feelings, and Oliver had a subtle, comforting presence.

Charlie just shrugged slightly. "But I've been learning so much more about my mom, about what her life was like before me," She looked at Amelie. "Apparently she and Oliver's mom were friends back in college."

"No shot," Amelie says looking at Oliver who nodded in agreement. "How come we didn't know this sooner, Oliver?"

Oliver shrugs. "I just found out. Mom doesn't talk much about her life outside of us," He paused "I guess my brothers and I never asked."

"That's sad," Amelie said. "I couldn't have kids because the second you're a mom that's all you are."

"What do you mean?" Oliver asked.

"Well think about it, when was the last time your mom did something for herself? What does she get for Christmas or her birthday? Stuff for the house, or for the family, right?" She points out "I mean you just learned that she was friends with your best friend's mom."

"Watch it," Oliver says lowly "It's not like you have deep conversations with your mom either."

"You watch it." Amelie shot back "Sorry my mom became a doctor and is out there doing good things for others. What does your mom do again?"

"Both of you knock it off!" Charlie exclaimed. "This is a ridiculous argument to be having."

Amelie sighs softly. "I'm sorry Oliver, I know your mom has a hard job raising you and your brothers. It wasn't right of me to say that."

Oliver pushed his hair back. "I'm sorry too. I shouldn't have said anything either, I know you don't like when she works often."

Amelie shrugs softly. "That's what life is. Working."

Oliver shakes his head "I don't think so. My mom would say she would rather be with us than work so much."

"Do you think your mom likes being a stay-at-home mom? Or was she made to?" Amelie paused "I'm not trying to start anything, I'm just curious." Her voice was softer now, showing no signs of judgment.

Oliver thought for a moment. "I know my dad would never make her do anything she didn't want to, he couldn't even if he wanted to. He loves her something fierce." He leans his arm against the table "I think my mom always wanted to be a mother; I think she was made for it really. In the sense that she loved picking out baby clothes and buying all the baby stuff. She has hundreds and hundreds of baby books. Always the loudest at all our sporting events," he chuckled

"She might've wanted a daughter at some point, but I don't think she would trade us for anything."

This sparked a thought in Charlie's brain. "Amelie, did your mother become a doctor because she wanted to?"

Amelie opened her mouth and then closed it for a moment. She would go to bat for her mother every time. But she knew Charlie didn't mean any disrespect. She never did. "My mother grew up with expectations," she says slowly. "Her parents always wanted her and her sister to be the best, do the best, and leave no room for anyone to question if you deserve your position." She chewed on her bottom lip. "My mom and aunt were supposed to be perfect. Appearance was everything. Hair, makeup, extracurriculars, and even friends were dictated by my grandma. I think it worked out for the best, Mom is a doctor, and my Aunt Amara is a lawyer."

"Does your mother like her job?" Charlie asked curiously.

Amelie looked at Charlie and stared at her for a moment. "We all have to do things for family, Charlie."

Chapter 17

Old Letter

Even though the park hang-out ended with a little tension, Charlie felt she had learned a lot. She noticed that Amelie was career driven. She believed that getting a good job where you earned a great salary was important. She was big on appearances, always making sure her hair was styled nicely, and was always showing a good front in public. Charlie couldn't think of a time when she had seen Amelie get angry or even cry in public. She did note that Amelie never wore her natural hair, always wearing it in braids, not yet adopting silk presses or wigs like her mother. Not that Charlie cared, she rarely even noticed, however, that got her wondering if her hairstyle was due to her mother's values.

Amelie did manage to let her personality shine through in other ways though, Charlie recounted. Amelie was a talented makeup artist. She didn't stick with natural makeup, opting for bold colors, and fun designs printed on her eyelids. Charlie wondered if that had been a fight between her and her mother. She concluded that even though Amelie loved the idea of being an event planner, the pressure to be the greatest was from her mother.

On the opposite side, Oliver seemed to believe that it didn't matter how much you made, but how much fun you had. He did well in school and did care about making a good living, but he was always doing things 'just because' as he put it. He went to all his soccer team's events made for team bonding even if they weren't mandatory. He went to as many concerts as he could during the summer, went to every school dance and was most likely going to be crowned homecoming king for junior prom, dabbled in musical instruments, went all out during school spirit days, and explored the outdoors every weekend with this family. Even his career choice of graphic designer was fun.

Oliver's parents were more of the average couple. They had a good relationship, they cared about their boys all equally. Oliver never complained about favoritism. His father worked a normal workweek, they had family dinner every night and they did family events every weekend. The only issue Charlie ever heard from them was when Oliver's father had gotten frustrated that Oliver would rather take an artistic path compared to his brothers who seemed to want to play every sport known to man.

Charlie remembered sitting in Oliver's room while he recalled the conversation he had had with his parents when he told his dad he didn't care to play all the sports that his brother had been into. He would continue with soccer, but he wanted to experience other things.

Recalling Oliver's retelling, his father had been confused, telling Oliver that he was skilled and that he had had a chance at getting scholarships and going to school for sports. Oliver pleaded his case that it wasn't something he wanted to continue to pursue. He wanted to experience more.

Charlie liked that about him. But it was also an attribute that confused her. She was fond of his enjoyment of exploration, and being the light of every room, however, always diving headfirst into things without a plan was a crazy concept to her. There were moments where she felt similar to Oliver, enjoying his carefree attitude towards things he enjoyed, and there were moments where she felt more similar to Amelie who had a plan for her life.

She began to think of the others in her life. Although she didn't have many deep talks with Uncle Aaron due to his busy work schedule, she did take note of the fact that he liked to provide. He was always working late, to make sure that his family was taken care of. It wasn't like the family was in a poor state, Skylar came from money, using it to spoil her kids, herself, and her husband rotten. However, Aaron still worked long days and late nights. Charlie believed that it was because a part of him enjoyed working.

Often, she found herself throwing herself into work when life seemed like an intolerable pressure on her head. On those days she would overachieve on her homework, offer to take care of her cousins more, and when she started working, she took more shifts. Anything to keep from dwelling in her thoughts. This did keep her from being social with her friends, but she figured she would much rather be her own reason for not being able to hang out than Skylar purposefully busying her with tasks.

There had been times when Skylar had known about events that Charlie wanted to attend and would "forget" and reserve a table at a restaurant for her and Aaron for a date. Neither one of the girls would tell Aaron that these dinners had not been planned with good intentions.

The more she thought about it, Skylar never seemed to like her. Well, she had when she was growing up, but after Victor was born, Charlie was nothing more than some kid at a family function. The realization of Aaron working late had plagued her mind when she had first moved in. She had moved in and now there were more mouths to feed. Logically Charlie knew that her alone wouldn't make a dent in financials, they had four children and Skylar came from money.

Logical thinking wasn't often on Charlie's side.

Charlie put Aaron and Amelie in the same category when it came to life. Work hard and provide even if it's tiring. Even if it wasn't what you want out of life.

Aaron hadn't wanted to work at his parent's store when he was younger, but he had to for the good of the family. Amelie might be all into event planning now, but for the longest time, she had wanted to go into cosmetology school. Charlie wouldn't say that these two are unhappy with their lives, but they seemed to be controlled by other forces.

Ms. Vivian on the other hand. Now that was something Charlie couldn't figure out. The woman was a mystery and seemed to like to stay that way. All Charlie knew was that Ms. Vivian was a teacher, looked after her mother growing up, never left Grand Fayword until impulsively deciding to pack up and move to New York to live with her best friend, and for some reason left an acorn keychain as a parting gift.

She still had no idea what that was about. She didn't want to go down that crisis spiral right now.

Ms. Vivian had given her great advice, even if it was disguised in puzzle-like wording. The meaning of the stories she told her often didn't click until later, usually when the girl was older.

Charlie had never thought to ask her about what she should be wanting from her life. She hadn't thought about asking her for career advice or what hobbies would best suit her. When she was with Ms. Vivian she just liked to be there. Listening to her stories and doing tasks around her house.

Ms. Vivian and Oliver were put in the same category. They both seemed carefree but not too much where they might go off the deep end.

Where did that leave her? She had a bit of Aaron's work ethic, and Amelie's planning, could she say she had Oliver and Ms. Vivian's carefree skills? Now she felt like contradicting herself. She took Aaron's work ethic and went overboard to the point it cost her moments with her friends. Unlike Amelie, she was an over-planner. She liked to know everything that was going to be happening, and when she didn't know what was possible, she would avoid that interaction altogether. The only time she felt like she could be like

Ms. Vivian and Oliver, was when she was around them. With her friends, she felt like she could push away any intrusive thoughts and just purely exist.

Charlie liked structure but wanted to want more from her life.

The girl got up from her bed and sat on the carpeted floor. She carefully reached under the bed and pulled out the mahogany box. Lifting the box carefully, she pushed around the contents before carefully lifting out the stack of envelopes.

Letters between her mother and Grayson.

Charlie had never wanted to read them for fear of invading privacy. However, there was a small part of her that felt like these letters could help her. Somehow. She wasn't sure how but there really was only one way of finding out. She picked out four at random from the stack, still feeling hesitant about opening all of them.

Carefully, she approached one of the letters as the precious item that it was. Her fingers gently hovered over the envelope, slowly peeling it back with a soft, careful motion. Her touch was light, wanting to avoid any damage to the delicate paper.

As the envelope's flap began to lift, she eased it open inch by inch, her fingers maintaining a steady support to prevent any strain on the paper. She held the paper carefully in her hands, paused briefly, then began to read.

Chapter 18

The Relentless School Cafeteria & Lily

My Dearest Lily,

I recall how after our first date you gushed about the main character writing letters for his significant other. I

must admit, I don't remember the movie in full, my attention was fully on you. Yes, that might sound

cliché but I can't help it. You wore a yellow dress and hoop earrings, and you put sparkles on your eyes.

Though those sparkles on your eyelids could never compete with the way your eyes shine. You are radiant,

my love. I am lucky enough to be in the same room as you, let alone be friends with you, to date you.

You would think that with the amount of writing experience, my penmanship would be stellar. However,

this is my third try. I can't begin to express the way you mean to me, but you want letters, and I would do anything

for you. Even if it is this simple act. One of these days you must let me take you on an extravagant date, my love. Something that measures up to the amazing woman that you are.

Though, I don't think it would be possible, I could try.

You know that I enjoy the movies with you, I even

enjoy eating lunch with you which makes the otherwise relentless school cafeteria much more bearable.

I hope this letter finds you well. I plan to slide it into your locker in the morning before school. I believe this method

seems easier than waiting for the postal service to deliver it to your house.

I hope this was what you had in mind when you thought of receiving written words of my admiration.

Say the word Lily and I will do my best to give you the world.

Yours,

Grayson

Chapter 19

Truly, Madly, Deeply, Always

Grayson,

I would be lying if I said this letter didn't find me at the right time, I was headed to Mr. B's math class. I would

also be lying if I said I didn't spend the first few moments of class giggling with my friends about my polished-

sounding boyfriend who wrote me the sweetest letter

(Don't worry my love, the contents of the letter remained only for you and me)

I have said it before but maybe it will help to have it in

writing. I don't need any extravagant dates, I enjoy just

being present with you. Even if it is in the "relentless"

cafeteria. However, I wouldn't mind a date with you

at Sunset Grove, they have my favorite chocolate lava cake and amazing pasta. I also would not be opposed

to having breakfast there, as their pancakes are to die for.

The only thing dates with me require are photos.

I have loved taking photos of important events

ever since I was a kid. I believe that taking pictures

makes the moments last longer and that

love is written all over them.

What do you say?

Lily

My love,

I am sorry that I have fallen off a bit with the letters,

but I hope that this will help you as we go through

Senior year. I am proud of you for getting a full

ride to Julliard. I know I have told you in person

but I thought you would get comfort in seeing

the words on paper so you can read them whenever

you need.

I always knew you were destined for great things

Lily May, and I do hope that I will be by your side

as you achieve them. I will be in the crowd cheering

loudly so that you never forget that you deserve the spotlight

I fell in love with a singer, and I would do anything to give

her a stage to perform on.

You are my forever.

Grayson

Lily,

I know you are married now. You have a daughter, and she is as beautiful as her mother. I know you are hurting, living with that man. I know how he treats you and how he disregards your accomplishments, your dreams, and all your mementos. I refuse to accept a world where a man can live my dream, disregard it, and call it unimpressive.

I want to take you away from here Lily. You and Charlie. You will bc safc; I promise you will not receive backlash from him. I will give you whatever it is your heart desires. I will build you a stage.

I did not want to risk mailing this letter and it falling into the wrong hands. So, I plan to slip this into Charlie's diaper bag while I am over-babysitting her.

I know for a fact Christopher won't find it there.

If you accept my offer, you know where to find me.

I love you, truly, madly, deeply, always

Grayson

Chapter 20

My Mother's Daughter

Henderson Household

How dare Oliver take a good game of volleyball and turn it into some kind of messed up therapy session? Amelie stormed up the steps of her porch and swung the front door open. She was moments from throwing her bag down and slamming the door when she noticed a pair of black clogs by the door.

Mom was home.

Amelie carefully let the door shut before slipping off her shoes. She hoisted her athletic drawstring bag over her shoulder and quietly moved up the stairs to her room. She put away her shoes in the closet and unpacked her bag, letting the volleyball roll into her closet while setting her water bottle down on her nightstand.

The search for her mother was now on, excited that she was home before nighttime. It was the perfect time for her to be home. Not too late that Amelie had gone to bed and not too early that the older woman wouldn't want a conversation. Amelie first checked her bedroom, the door was open which was a good indication that her mother was not in there. If it had been closed the idea of talking to her mother would be immediately shot down.

Next, she checked the most logical place, since the front door had led into the living room and Amelie hadn't seen her, she went to the kitchen. She made her way into the kitchen and saw her mother sitting in one of the dining chairs. "Hey Mom," Amelie said softly.

Angela Henderson had her head in her hands, her straightened hair slightly tousled from hours under a surgical mask. Her black locks fall gently past her shoulders, showing signs of a long day but still carrying the soft, silky quality that defines her style. A few strands might be slightly out of place, but overall, her hair frames her face with a relaxed elegance. The woman let out a soft grunt of acknowledgment but didn't give more than that.

Amelie carefully took a seat in a chair across from her. "I played volleyball with Oliver and Charlie today" Before she could mention that her skills were still polished and she hadn't been beaten by Oliver, her mother spoke.

"Have you been working on your college essays?"

Amelie was taken back a bit, "Oh uhm yeah. I worked on them"

Angela just nodded before lifting her head and reaching for the glass of water next to her. She took a slow sip and looked out the window to the right of her.

"Did you get ahold of Dad yet? I wanted to tell him about my internship"

Amelie's father was a lawyer and had currently been out of town for business. He promised both of them that he would check in when he could.

"I've been at work since last night Amelie," she said.

"I know."

"He's been working."

"Yes, ma'am I know."

"He isn't on a personal trip, work is his main focus right now," she sets her glass down "I'm sure you could understand that, even as an… event planner." Her tone was evidence of how she felt about her daughter's planned profession.

It had nearly taken blood, sweat, and tears from Amelie just to convince her parents that event planning was something that she could achieve, something that was a livable profession. She had created a PowerPoint listing demographics, which locations are suitable for planners, their salary, the success rate, and her own achievements that would qualify her to be a good planner.

That didn't even satisfy her mother, her father not having anything against it since it wouldn't easily make his daughter hungry on the streets, so Amelie had to speak to her grandparents about it. They didn't seem to care as they were done parenting and had moved on to the fun grandparents, much to Angela's dismay. Only then did she begrudgingly agree.

"I thought it was better than going to cosmetology school," Amelie mumbled softly looking down at the table runner, not daring to look at her mother for this conversation.

Angela scoffs. "It doesn't mean it's good enough. Your father and I work long hours, late nights, to bring home money so you can have whatever you want. We went to school and studied hard so that we could take care of ourselves and our future family," She straightened up "You are lucky I let you spend time with your friends after school, I was nicer than my parents."

"I don't think that having friends is supposed to be a reward. I think it's what parents usually strive for their kids to have." She glanced up and met her mother's brown eyes.

"I think parents usually strive for their kid not to be a smart mouth who wants to throw away her talents for some lousy internship."

"I'm not throwing away anything! I'm good at event planning and it's fun!"

"A good job isn't always about fun!" She shot back "You are an incredibly smart girl, I thought you were going to follow in our footsteps. Everyone in our family is something great. Doctors, Lawyers, CEO's. I'm not sure where I went wrong."

Amelie didn't let that comment get to her, it wasn't even the first time she heard her mother gripe about her daughter not wanting to follow in anyone else's path. "You're saying you don't enjoy your job?"

Angela's face darkened. "I didn't say that. Don't put words in my mouth."

"I'm not," Amelie said softly. "I just. I know you like your job, you did it for a reason. You wanted to help people," She paused "Dad said you wanted to be a therapist."

She scoffed and rolled her eyes at the mention of her old career aspiration. "I wanted to be at first sure, but your grandmother told me I couldn't make a lot of money that way. I chose doctor, that way everyone was happy."

Amelie felt saddened at the thought of a young Angela being told that she couldn't have the job she wanted because it didn't make enough money. "Why did the money matter so much?"

She stood up, tired of this conversation. "You want less money? We gave you everything!"

"I wanted you guys!" She says standing up. "You guys were always working. I just wanted you guys to come to my games and visit for career day."

Angela huffs. "Telling children about the jobs we do isn't a good enough reason to take off work."

"But you do care about other people's perception."

Angela scoffs. "Not enough or else I wouldn't let you go off to this internship and throw your life away."

"You're not proud of me?"

Angela walked to the sink and set her cup there "I could be prouder if there was anything worth being proud of." She left the kitchen and went to her bedroom shutting the door.

Amelie stood alone in the kitchen for a moment before going to her room. She grabbed a notebook and a pastel pink pen before sitting down at her desk. Opening to a fresh page she started to write, although her letters were slightly uneven in size and slant, her idea was clear. "Plan To Get Charlie Uncursed"

She drew little stars that marked the bulleted list she was starting to create. She tapped her pen against her desk while thinking. Trying to get Charlie motivated with a career by making her take a personality test did not work. The girl had not wanted to leave so she needed some kind of plan to show Charlie that there was something out there that was worth leaving Grand Fayword for.

Almost immediately she remembered the last conversation she had with Charlie at the park. She quickly scribbled something down.

Research Grayson

Chapter 21

Committing Crimes For Friendship

"Man, I sure do love spending my holiday break stalking people," Oliver said slightly bored.

"Shut up Oliver," Amelie mumbled while typing quickly on her laptop keyboard.

The group was sitting at a table in the back of the library. Amelie had proposed a crazy scheme to find Grayson, Lily's boyfriend, for some odd reason that Charlie and Oliver were not quite sure of.

"Well, I do think it's stalking, besides, you don't even know his last name. How are you going to find the right one?" He countered.

"I would have a way easier time if Charlie would just tell me his last name."

Charlie didn't budge, she didn't want to go digging up the past. She also didn't think finding Grayson made any sense. If she told Amelie his last name, she would find him online, and then what? Message him? Find his address? That was definitely going into stalker territory. "I propose we talk about how crazy it is that school gives us an entire week off to "celebrate our town's history" I mean what's up with that?"

"It wouldn't be Grand Fayword if we didn't have grand gestures," Oliver pointed out "Our break started normally with celebrating

Halloween and then Vivian moves away, Charlie gets cursed, and Amelie wants to commit a felony. Grand!"

"You are not helping." Amelie snapped.

The two stopped talking and glanced at each other. It was easy to notice that Amelie had been a little on edge recently. Charlie couldn't exactly figure out why, it made sense that she cared about Charlie's well-being, but she had seemed more intense with it now.

Amelie took a deep breath and slowly let it out before speaking. "Listen, I can't change your mind about where you want to go to school or what you want as a career, but I won't sit here and be okay with the fact that you are just going to be stuck here. I mean you can't even come to visit me if you wanted" She shrugs "So I thought maybe if we found where Grayson was, you could go find him and maybe learn more about your mom. That has got to be motivation enough."

Charlie stared at her for a long moment, there was too much going on in her brain for her to formulate anything. She wanted to debate her, get up and leave, be sad, or maybe even offended. But what if she was right? Charlie had always wanted to know more about her mom, it was hard to talk to Aaron about it and Ms. Vivian had left, so maybe if she found Grayson and if he even wanted to see her… There was a small chance.

"Kingsley," She says quietly "Grayson Kingsley."

"Thank you, Charlie," Amelie replied before typing away on her laptop again.

The next 10 minutes were filled with verbal silence. Amelie had been typing away, not sharing any of her findings yet. Oliver had been given the task of painting Charlie's nails with a deep green polish Amelie had found in her bag. Anything to keep his hands busy. Charlie was sitting staring off into the distance creating a scenario in her head of what it would be like to meet Grayson.

Of course, she wasn't sure what he would look like now so the only image she could create was the ones she had taken from the photos. A young Grayson Kingsley, with his hair styled neatly, and dressed in a suit had opened the door to his, most likely, expensive, lavish mansion. He recognized her immediately, ushered her inside and sat with her on his expensive-looking couch. He would go on and on about her mother, how he loved her and how he wished he had come back for her.

Why hadn't he come back for her?

Charlie had snapped out of her thoughts with an anxious pit in her stomach. Grayson had to have a reason for never coming back to rescue her mother away from this town, away from her relationship with Christopher. So why didn't he? Charlie was about to tell Amelie to stop searching to call it off. But she was too late.

"Found him!" Amelie whipped around her laptop to display an elegant-looking website. A business page. "Well, I couldn't find him,

I don't think he has a social media page, but I did find where his company is located."

Charlie sat forward to better see the screen, earning a quiet 'Careful Now' from Oliver who had started nail painting on her left hand. Her eyes trailed over to him, for the first time since being out of her head she noticed how carefully he had been gliding the brush over her nail beds, how focused he looked never seeming this focused before, and how gently he held her hand.

It took Charlie a moment to come back to reality and look at the screen again. In big black letters at the top of the page, it read "Kingsley Wellness Clinic". She scrolled down and read over their mission statement. "They are a behavior health clinic that offers same-day access for those in a mental health crisis," Charlie read. "They offer a ton of services as well as housing to get people back on their feet."

"Wait, you said that Grayson didn't want to go work with his father and the family business," Oliver pointed out "Wouldn't that make him... a bad person?"

"See I remembered Charlie talking about that, so I did some more research and there is another company called "Kinsley Crest Vineyards" whose owner looks like…" She reaches over and opens another tab pulling up the Vineyards website.

A picture of two men, one was tall, with white hair and muted blue eyes, he wore a tailored charcoal gray suit, and the other man was almost a spitting image of Grayson. However, this man's hair was styled differently, the back and sides were faded but his front was left longer it had a smooth, sweeping effect, where the hair seemed brushed back with a slight curve.

"I think Grayson started at the family business and then left to start his own. His younger brother Michael taking his place. Another possibility is that maybe Grayson was replaced by his brother. I'm not sure," Amelie clicked back to the other tab "But this Clinic is located in Riverstone, North Carolina"

"North Carolina," Charlie mumbled softly her fingers lightly grazing the mouse pad as she scrolled down, careful not to smudge her freshly painted nails, until she found an *About Us* tab. She clicked on it hoping she would see a picture of Grayson—something for her to hold on to, to keep this insane idea afloat. Unfortunately, there was no picture of him at all. There was barely anything written about him. His name was listed as the *Founder*, but the only other information was about the staff and how the clinic strives to strengthen the community.

"So?" Amelie spoke up gently. She looked at Charlie as if she were a shy toddler who was not ready to leave her mother for daycare. "Do you think we should go find him?"

"Amelie that's not fair. We don't have a plan, we can't just load up a car and head to North Carolina." Oliver objected, quickly being met with a glare from the girl.

"I am not saying we leave now but I want Charlie to know she has options outside of staying here," She scoffs. "Now go back to painting her nails. We're talking here"

He rolled the closed nail polish container back over to her. "I'm finished and I think this color looks nice on her. Thanks for asking"

"I want to go," Charlie spoke up.

Oliver blinked at her.

Amelie grinned excitedly and started packing up. "Perfect! I really think this is going to work Char!"

Charlie was less enthusiastic but nodded and stood up.

The walk to the edge of town wasn't that long but it felt like it dragged on. Thoughts and expectations swirled around in her brain like the fall winds swirled around the leaves on the ground as they walked. She was going to meet Grayson. Someone that played some part in her childhood, and a big part in her mother's life. He had seemed to be a good guy in Ms. Vivian's stories, and in the letters, and wanting to dedicate his resources and time to help others only added to that presumption.

There wasn't any doubt that Grayson wouldn't like her. It wasn't like she was going there in hopes of becoming a part of his life. She had questions about her mother, and he could answer them.

If she could know about her mother, then she could know about herself.

They came up to the edge of town. The stretch of trees and the white sign. She took it all in and thought about finally getting her life figured out just like everyone else had. Her thoughts subsided when she felt a hand on her back, she looked over at Oliver who gave her a small smile.

"You don't have to do this," He whispers softly remembering how devastated Charlie was the last time they had been here.

"No, I want to," Charlie nods "I need to know."

Oliver just nodded and looked over at Amelie who was a little ways ahead of them.

"Let's go guys. We're gonna take a walk while we figure out a plan to find Grayson," She turns her head to look at Charlie "You hear that? We're gonna go out of town just to think of a plan and we will come back"

Charlie logically knew they weren't walking to North Carolina, that would be insane. She figured Amelie was saying this aloud as if she was convincing the curse to let her friend go.

Amelie took a few steps and passed the white welcome sign. She turned around and waved to the others before continuing to walk slowly.

Oliver hesitated, his eyes stayed on Charlie trying his best to read her facial expression. Looking for any hint that she wanted this to stop. He would stop it if he could. If she wanted him to. When she hadn't looked away from where Amelie was, he decided to make his way as well. He stood by Amelie and turned to Charlie.

Charlie nodded to herself, took a deep breath, and started walking. She thought of her mom and how she was close to figuring her out. She could meet up with Ms. Vivian and excitedly tell her that she had become whole again and had meaning. Her life would fall into place, and everyone would be happy with her.

"Charlie!" Amelie's tone of voice was a mix of frustration and sadness.

Charlie wasn't sure why; she had looked around and noticed she hadn't moved at all. Still stuck at the beginning, though she was sure she had started moving to her friends. Again, she started walking towards the trees, towards the sign, towards her friends, towards what she needed.

Instantly she felt that static-like feeling against her skin, there was no pain, but it was noticeable. It felt like walking into an invisible barrier, a brief sensation of resistance. The curse was not broken. She was stuck here.

"Why didn't that work!" Amelie groans tiredly. "I don't understand."

Frustration begins to cloud Charlie's expression. Her first attempts to push through were a determined but futile effort. She presses her hands against the invisible barrier, fingers splaying out in a vain attempt to break through the unseen wall. The resistance is firm and unyielding, and her face tightens with a growing sense of helplessness.

“I get that you want to stay and be a librarian. Whatever, you like books and organization and routine and I never questioned it cause that’s just how you are Charlie,” Amelie kept going. “I never understood you, you hate new things and change but you don’t have any plan in place?!”

Charlie’s frustration builds quickly, turning to anger as she pounds her fists against the forcefield. Each hit is met with a soft, reverberating thud, the impact bouncing back with a disheartening lack of give. Her movements become more erratic, breathing more labored, as if the barrier itself is mocking her desperation. The once silent area now echoes with the sound of her futile strikes and Amelie’s harsh words.

“I thought that finding the only guy to ever love your mother would be enough to wake something up inside of you!” her voice grew more expressive. “But not even that is worth leaving. Why don’t you want to get out of here!”

“Amelie stop it!” Oliver interjected but was pointless over the sounds of Charlie’s struggle and Amelie’s words.

“What is wrong with you? Why do you have to hurt others by being so stubborn!” Amelie screams.

Driven by mounting despair, Charlie escalates her efforts. She turns and runs at full force, charging towards the barrier with a desperate, wild energy. Her body hits the forcefield with a jarring impact, a surge of adrenaline fueling her attempts to break free. The collision sends a shockwave of frustration through her, the invisible wall remaining resolute and unbroken. She slams against it repeatedly, shoulders and chest pressing hard as she bangs on the barrier with increasingly frantic energy.

Amelie kept going, the words falling out of her mouth faster than she could think. "We just want to help you and you're not trying! Everyone you love will not stay here and you'll be all alone! Why don't you understand that?!"

"I'm trying!" Charlie's voice cracked as her repeated impacts left her breathless and exhausted. Her face flushed with tears mingling with sweat as her efforts became more disheartened and less coordinated. Each strike felt less like a physical effort and more like an emotional outburst, the frustration of being trapped merging with a deep, aching sadness. The forcefield stands unmoved, leaving her slumped against it, overwhelmed by the realization of her confinement.

Oliver rushed over seeing Charlie's exhausted body slumping against the force field. His heart ached at the sight of Charlie's raw frustration and exhaustion. He starts to speak calmly, trying to cut through the haze of anger and sadness. "Hey, it's okay. You'll be okay," he says softly, reaching out a hand to her.

Charlie looks up, eyes red and filled with a mixture of relief and frustration. The contrast between her anger and the calm demeanor of Oliver seems almost palpable.

"We are done here Amelie," Oliver gently guided Charlie away from the barrier, leading her to a spot where she could sit down.

"No. No, I'm not done." Amelie said following them. "I want to know why you don't want to leave."

"I do Amelie," Charlie reassured her, almost begging her. "I hate that all my classmates know exactly what they want to do with their life! Yes, I know I am insufferable for always wanting a routine and for not doing anything new but that doesn't mean I know a plan for my life." She laughed tiredly "I wish my brain worked that way."

"Why can't you think of something better to do than be a librarian."

Charlie thought for a moment, trying to catch her breath and think of a way to explain this in a way that would make sense to Amelie. "Why did you give up convincing your parents to be a cosmetologist?"

"...What?"

"You wanted to go to school for cosmetology, and now you're an event planner."

"People can change their minds on careers Charlie."

"Sure, but this didn't seem like it. You were excited to tell your parents about your passion. You had a whole presentation prepared. You came back to school the next day... sort of distant."

"That's all that was. A passion." She scoffs "Not a solid plan. I like event planning"

"Your passion could be a solid career, Amelie. But you chose to change, which there is nothing wrong with. However, I know for a fact that your mother gave you a list of other occupations to choose from. I know you went back and forth with her before you found something that interested you and put her concern of a livable salary at ease."

Amelie hadn't said anything. Charlie was right, that was how a lot of her conversations with her mother went, Angela shot things down and Amelie found some sort of compromise.

"I know you weren't happy with your choice until you were given an internship," She clocked the look of realization in her friend's eyes. "You had been worried, and winging all the other events you had put together. Only feeling at peace when it seemed like this random idea would fall into place."

Amelie rolled her eyes and crossed her hands. "This has nothing to do with me. I want to leave this place, you don't."

"I don't have a reason to," she whispers softly "I don't have someone pushing me in one direction or another. I can't stumble into a career as a result of rebelling against someone." She paused "I love you guys, and I will miss you terribly, but I just thought that if I could find out about my mom. Find Grayson. That I could find out more about me. About who I am. I don't know anything about my parents or who they wanted me to be. I don't know who I want to be"

Amelie was quiet for a moment, staring at Oliver who hadn't taken his eyes off Charlie, and who was still crouched down with his hand on her shoulder. "So, you want someone to tell you what to do then?" She asked. "You want to live a life where your mother is constantly telling you that she's disappointed in you for not picking a better path?"

"Amelie," Oliver warns.

"No Oliver. This is what she wants. She wants to disappoint her father for not following in his footsteps and going to his college on a football scholarship." She caught the hurt in his eyes and whipped her head back to look at Charlie. "I don't know why you're upset that you have no one telling you what to do. I had a whole plan that was just wasted because of my mother! And her mother! and her mother's mother!"

"Amelie knock it off already!" Oliver stood up.

"We all have to do things we don't like to do! Better get to pretending Charlie because that's what the real world is about! You either are forced to follow in your parent's footsteps or disappoint them." She paused for half a second, but it wasn't long enough to consider the consequences "Or you forget who you are as a person and feel compelled to follow in your husband's wishes"

Charlie felt her heart sink. She had almost regretted that night at the park when she told them that she had learned about her father, that he had controlled her mother. Regretted telling them about Grayson.

"That is enough Amelie!" Oliver had never raised his voice before. He usually was filled with emotion when he spoke but this time, he had almost yelled at her. "You have gone too far, I should've stopped you earlier, but I thought you would've heard your own words and realized you're being a jerk!" He held up his hand as Amelie was about to speak "You've done enough talking. Now you can feel however you want about Charlie and her decisions. Even if Charlie doesn't go to school anywhere else it will not be the end of your friendship, what will be the end of your friendship is you pushing her to do what she doesn't want to do."

Amelie stopped, she looked between both of them and just scoffed. She shook her head and walked off.

Oliver looked down at Charlie and sat back down with her "Let's just sit for a moment" he said quietly.

Charlie's breathing begins to slow as she focuses on Oliver's steady presence. A softness in her eyes now, a glimmer of trust as she leans into the comfort being offered. She allows herself to find comfort in his warmth and understanding.

Chapter 22

Just A Girl

Henderson Household

There was no one home when Amelie stormed inside. She threw her stuff in the living room and bolted up the stairs to her room. She flung the door open and tried to slam it shut but it had gotten caught by a volleyball.

She screamed in frustration and threw the ball, before turning to her door and slamming it hard. The reverberation of the door slamming echoed through the quiet house, a testament to her raw frustration. For a moment, she stood there, fuming, her eyes darted toward the door, her anger not yet spent.

With a growl, she swung the door open again, this time letting it slam even harder, the frame rattling under the impact. She barely waited for the door to swing back before slamming it shut once more, the noise punctuating the air like a drumbeat of her exasperation.

Each time she opened and slammed the door, the sound grew louder, more jarring, until it seemed to fill the entire house. Her movements became more frantic as if the door was a punching bag for her pent-up emotions. The repeated banging was relentless, a physical manifestation of the anger swirling inside her.

Finally, she flung the door open one last time and leaned against the doorframe, her breaths heavy and uneven. The room fell into an uneasy silence, broken only by the occasional creak of the door swinging slightly on its hinges. Amelie stood there, her shoulders heaving as she tried to calm herself, the door now a silent witness to the storm she'd unleashed.

Slowly she let herself sink to the ground and covered her face with her hands. She brought her knees to her chest but did not cry. She could not think of the last time she had let herself cry, her parents never really showed emotion that way. Well, her mother never did, she would throw herself into work and come home filled with all the emotions she held bottled up through the day.

Her mother was a good doctor, kind and caring, but all that emotion got spent, barely any being saved for her daughter. Surprisingly though, her parents' relationship was fine. Her father was good at communicating and good at helping his wife with her own communication. He was hardly around when his daughter was in the path of her mother's anger.

Amelie turned her head and stared at the door that had just received all of her anger. She wished she could say that she felt bad for what she had done in her angry outburst, but she kind of enjoyed it. There was so much emotion in her that she felt a little lighter to let it go somewhere.

She looked straight ahead and caught sight of her reflection in the mirror. Her face was flushed, and the intricate braids that tumbled down her back now seemed a bit disheveled, some strands escaping their neat pattern. She reached up absently, smoothing them with a touch that felt more mechanical than intentional. Her mother would be ashamed.

Her hazel eyes echoed the same tired glint of her mother's as she stared into her own gaze, there was a moment of quiet, a pause where the intensity of her earlier anger softened into a more contemplative silence.

Her face, caught between the lingering traces of anger and the beginnings of calm, showed a vulnerable honesty.

Despite all her anger, she was still just a girl all alone.

Gently, she reached over and shut the door before crawling over and lying in the middle of her room. She looked up at her ceiling, catching sight of the glow-in-the-dark stars that a young Amelie and Charlie had put up.

Why was Charlie being so stubborn? All she wanted to do was help her figure out her life. She had given her so many options, but she seemed so content with just staying here. She didn't care about having a job that wasn't the same one from high school, she didn't care about leaving here. Charlie needed a passion or a reason for wanting to leave. But she didn't want a different job, nor did she want to travel anywhere. But then why wasn't the hunt for Grayson a good enough reason to break the curse?

Her mind started to drift back to the stars on the ceiling. Her mother had gotten upset with her for "messing up her ceiling," but her father had said it was no big deal and that she was just a kid.

Amelie wondered now what it was like when her mother was a kid. She knew that her mother did not have it easy, and that Amelie suffered the same fate as a young Angela. *'My mom never did that for me so why should I do that for you?'* was often what Amelie heard growing up. It often felt that her mother had been getting back at her own, but the only one hurting in this scenario was Amelie.

Charlie was right. Amelie had wanted to be a cosmetologist but only decided on event planning because she could still have some creative range. She worried that she was not going to be good at it, that she would fail and be forced to be a doctor or lawyer. But thankfully, Claire Carter had given her an internship at Lifestyle Event Planning, and Amelie could see the light at the end of the tunnel. She had been pretending since Sophomore year, had thrown herself into school clubs like STUCO, and gotten a job at the library in hopes of being able to plan events, just so she could prove to others and herself that she would not become like her mother or stuck at a job she didn't want.

This situation was a win-lose scenario. She liked event planning, but she had given up her real passion for her mother's sake. That hadn't even gotten her approval. Angela was still not proud of her.

Amelie sat up slowly. She had treated Charlie just like she had been treated by her mother. She had tried to help by making Charlie do whatever Amelie thought was best. And when Charlie showed any hint of being her own person, Amelie got angry and accused her of not trying or not caring.

Amelie wanted the best for Charlie. She had wanted to be the one to help break this curse, but she was not what Charlie needed. How could she be when she couldn't even break herself free?

Chapter 23

Acorns & The Color Blue

Charlie had shaken off the event that transpired back by the edge of town. She had reassured Oliver that she was fine and just needed a moment alone.

Now, she walked down the quiet streets of Grand Fayword, she made sure to stick to back roads so she wouldn't be interrupted by the town life on the main streets. She wanted a moment to collect her thoughts and work through why the curse hadn't been broken.

Going to meet Grayson clearly hadn't been the answer, which was a small relief. She wasn't sure she could face someone who had taken care of her yet hadn't come back for her. The girl was already having trouble figuring herself out, she didn't want to divulge in the mess that was her mother's love life.

A bit frustrated, she shoved her hands in her jacket pocket and that's when she felt something. She pulled out the small, wooded acorn on a silver keychain. The gift from Ms. Vivian. Somehow in all this stress of the curse and learning about her mother, she had forgotten about this acorn.

This stupid acorn that had sent her down this spiral. She had been completely fine before she had been given this thing. She was content with living here forever, but this stupid acorn was the reason she started to feel like she was missing out, that she needed to figure herself out.

Charlie refused to admit that she had always felt those feelings. That this search was a last desperate attempt to find the answers. Her mother's letters had been of no help and the journal didn't help either. It was clear through the six pages that she had read that Lily was just as lost.

She held the keychain between her fingers and watched it sway. Her thoughts kept circling back to Ms. Vivian, and how she missed her. There was no way to communicate as the older lady only had a landline and Charlie didn't know her new address. She wondered if she could find Dezi Carver's business address and send a letter that way. There was no concrete plan, all she knew was that she needed to talk to Ms. Vivian.

The feelings grew stronger, an unshakable certainty that Ms. Vivian was on her mind for a reason. It was more than just a thought; it was as though a quiet voice within was urging her, a subtle pull that she couldn't ignore. Her intuition began to nudge her toward home as if the two thoughts were intertwined. The sense of urgency was soft but persistent, like a whisper that seemed to grow louder with each passing moment.

Her heart raced as she sprinted through her town, each step propelling her closer to home. The asphalt beneath her feet felt solid and reassuring, the familiar texture of the ground smoothing out her frantic energy. The neatly lined sidewalks and well-tended lawns flashed by in a blur, but her focus remained steadfast on the promise of answers waiting for her.

The sun was beginning to set, casting a warm, golden glow over the town, and making the air feel fresh and invigorating. The smooth pavement beneath her seemed to vibrate with her anticipation, each footfall a reminder of the joy and relief she felt. The quiet hum of the town's evening life and the gentle rustle of leaves in the breeze added to the sense of urgency and excitement that drove her forward.

Her face was lit up with a smile, reflecting the happiness that surged through her. The feeling of the ground underfoot, the soft warmth of the fading sunlight, and the cozy familiarity of her surroundings all contributed to the lightness in her step. As she neared her home, the world around her narrowed to the simple, exhilarating truth that she was on the verge of finding the answers she had been looking for.

Finally reaching her front yard, she slowed to a stop, her smile slightly faded as she was met with the sight of Amelie on her porch. The feeling that was begging her to go home had faded. Stupidly she believed that she had the answers, that Ms. Vivian had come back to help her.

Amelie must have sensed that she was being watched because her head lifted and turned towards Charlie. "Hey Char," She spoke softly

Charlie didn't respond, just carefully made her way to the porch, opting to stand on the steps instead of sitting next to Amelie.

"I know that there is no apology or excuse I can give you that will make up for the way I treated you," She says quickly "I messed up badly. I was so upset and because of that, I treated you the only way I knew how to react when things weren't going my way. I was trying to force you to act how I thought you should act. It's how my mom treats me and I just… I follow her rules with little to no questions and I was upset by the fact that you could so easily make your own decisions."

Charlie laughed softly at that. "Amelie, I am searching through the things of my mother, who is no longer here, in order to get some kind of guidance. I can't make my own decisions."

"But you didn't care about things like status when picking out a job or a college. You just did what you originally liked to do. You need someone who can help you in the way that you need. I can't do that for you."

Charlie thought for a moment before sighing softly "I know I can be a bit hard to deal with."

"You're not," Amelie says quickly.

Charlie nodded "Even I think so. I just want my brain to be like everyone else's," She chuckled softly. "I hate that I like structure to the point where things crumble if I don't have it. I hate that it seems like everyone else is understanding this secret language, but I'm left in the dark." She takes a deep breath, her fingers gently twisting the ring around her finger. "Sometimes it makes people think I don't care about them, but I do. I care a lot more than I can really say. It all just feels like I'm not in control of my life or my own thoughts most of the time"

Amelie was quiet for a moment, not having any answers for her. Her mind went over scenarios where it seemed that Charlie was out of control, pestering to leave for the pet store right at 1:30 like Amelie had said, instead of two minutes after. The argument the girls had when Amelie asked her why she was in such a bad mood and not talking to her. She didn't understand when Charlie told her she wasn't mad, she just didn't want to talk, just wanted to listen. Amelie didn't believe her, instead she got mad and ignored her. It didn't help anything, just led to tension and Amelie going home early.

Amelie knew she wasn't going to have the answers. She felt bad for thinking she had known Charlie the best, just to treat her badly when she had needed someone the most. "I get it you know, wanting some guidance from your mom."

Charlie sat down next to her "Yeah?"

"I get so angry with my mother for not listening to me, but that's all I want. Her to listen to me, hold me, and guide me." She looks down at her hands.

"You don't have to follow her plan for your life."

Amelie gave a short nod "I know. But I'm going to do it anyway. It's all I've ever known, and the closest I have ever gotten to a real connection to my mother is following whatever plan she has for me."

The girls were quiet for a moment, just staring at the sun as it started to set, sinking behind the houses. It was a comfortable silence. Charlie's mind was quiet, and it didn't feel like she wanted to crawl out of her skin. Amelie wasn't beating herself up for the problems she caused and wasn't thinking of her next steps. Both girls were content in the moment.

"I love you, Amelie," Charlie reassured her after a moment.

Amelie was quiet for a moment, a small smile on her face as she stared ahead of her "I promise to keep an open room for you when you decide to leave Grand Fayword."

Maybe Ms. Vivian was right about Charlie just being like her. Ms. Vivian had her Dezi Carver and Charlie had her Amelie Henderson.

It was late and Amelie had gone home. Charlie went to her room to get ready for bed, she shut her bedroom door behind her and made her way to her dresser to take off her ring. That's when she noticed the blue envelope with her name written on it, sitting propped up nicely waiting for her.

Aaron must have gotten mail while she was out. It was strange, Charlie had never gotten letters before. She opened it with the same care that she had opened her mother's letters, and started to read:

Charlie,

I was once told that I was wise, smart, and thoughtful, and for some reason that reminded them of the color blue. English class later taught me that blue often symbolizes a quest for inner understanding. I thought that was just plain dumb because I didn't think of myself as wise, and I sure didn't have any kind of inner understanding. I was just like you, I didn't know what I wanted to do with my life, I believed that life was just working until you died, so I didn't put any effort into the things I did. I didn't go to college and got a mediocre job at a grocery store. That is when the curse found its home in me, but I didn't care. My peers had all moved on and what I thought was content with my life soon revealed itself as denial. My best friend Dezi Carver had sent me a letter detailing her new job in the fashion world, she reminded me that I reminded her of the color blue.

I don't know what it was but one day I woke up and decided to give myself a chance. I went to school and became a teacher (I was inspired by my 3rd-grade teacher) I started teaching and fell in love with it. I loved all my students and everything they taught me

I didn't care about lifting the curse anymore because I was happy with my job. Then one day I met a radiant, scatterbrained girl, who I had the pleasure of teaching and being able to watch grow. That girl eventually taught me that there was more to life than I had thought. I watched this girl deny everything good to herself and I realized that I had seen myself in her.

I saw myself in her and I saw that in you Charlie. I did not want you to be like me. I gave you that acorn key chain as a reminder. Just like acorns you have potential, are strong, and always have room for growth. Even the smallest beginnings can lead to great achievements. I wanted this acorn key chain to encourage you to embrace your unique gifts and talents. Like you, I believed that I had to do something great in order to be living life. I had no strong urge to "cement my name in history" so I was content with living here, but I had missed so much.

I had been reminded of that girl after recalling countless stories of her, I then decided, finally that I was ready to see what was in store for me, to break away from the narrative that I was put here to do something, that is too big of an expectation, I decided I was put here just to live. Now, I had a feeling that the curse would be passed down to you for the same reasons. I can't tell you how to live, baby, you have to figure that out for yourself.

I wanted to stop denying myself fun experiences just because I was scared. Life is scary but being a little scared means, you are living it. You can't play it safe forever… Remember that.

For when you are ready:

333 Willow Creek Lane

Evergreen Heights, EH 45678

United States

Charlie held the letter in her hand and slowly sunk down into her desk chair. Ms. Vivian had been cursed as well, Amelie had been right. If Vivian was like Charlie, that had meant that at some point Ms. Vivian was also scared of how put together her peers seemed, she found the most generic job that would accept her, and she pretended to herself and everyone that this was what she had wanted and that she was content.

She glanced at the letter again and noticed an address, she assumed it was where Ms. Vivian had moved. That was rather pointless to her now, so she didn't pay too much attention to it.

Her mother hadn't had life figured out, neither had Ms. Vivian. Amelie was pretending to have it all together as well, so who was she supposed to turn to? She still didn't have many answers for how to break her curse. The letter said that worrying about being remembered throughout history was a waste of time and to stop denying oneself fun experiences. But Ms. Vivian couldn't even tell her the answers. Amelie could only tell her from her own twisted experiences, and her mother, her poor mother, continued to deny herself everything she wanted.

Part of her wanted to throw the letter and the journal in a box shove it under her bed and pretend like it didn't exist. Finish out her school year, attend college here, and figure out a way to be content with being cursed. But the other part, the part screaming at her, kept thinking about her mother. Her mother had so much in store for her, she had someone who truly loved her, and she had a career waiting for her, but she let go of all of it, let it slip through her fingers for people who had their own lives to live. Ms. Vivian walked shakily on the line between denial and wanting something great, that she had almost gotten to the other side but deep down still believed she wasn't doing enough. Amelie was willingly walking down the same path as her mother, trying to please everyone and change something that she couldn't control.

What was she even supposed to do? No one knew the answers. She felt foolish for thinking that if she had known about her mother, that she could have figured herself out. She felt dumb for picking the first career option on a personality test, yeah, she loved it, but it was making her feel stuck.

"Drive myself mad trying to find my reason for being here or drive myself mad wondering if staying here is all I am destined for?" she mumbled aloud.

Who had put it in her head that she needed a reason to be worthy of existing?

Developing a migraine, Charlie had decided to be done with this existential spiral for the time being. She put the letter back in its envelope and decided to keep it safe in her mother's journal. She flipped to the seventh page, thinking it would be empty, but realized she had missed a whole entry.

Lily's Journal Page 7

Charlie Grayce May,

You had not even been born yet, but I had already had your name picked out. You are keeping my last name because you are my heart. I did not wish to bring you into this world with any real ties to Christopher. He wasn't there for your birth, he is barely around to help take care of you, so why should he get a say in your name?

I am not going to fill this page with any more things Christopher has done. I will not fill the rest of this with what has gone on in my life, with my family. I want to write to you though I don't plan on ever showing you this. If I find this advice fitting, I will tell it to you myself. I want our family to share and be close. We won't run like an operation.

I saw Grayson. He came to see me and was so good to you. He had been sending me money even after I told him that it was no longer needed~~ and that my brother nor I could handle taking care of the business anymore. He~~ offered to watch over you, and I happily agreed. He would've made an amazing father.

~~He told me he wanted to take me with him. He wanted to start a life with me and my daughter. I cried when I told him I couldn't leave. That Christopher would be looking for me. I was a bit emotional when I told him the only way out of here was to run away and go~~

~~into hiding. I couldn't go on the run with a baby, Aaron could take her. Gray knew I was just upset. I would never leave my baby.~~

I take back what I said about no one benefiting from my experiences. My wish for my daughter is to never feel the pressure that I did. I spent so much of my time trying to figure out what I wanted to do that I almost missed out on experiences that made me truly happy.

I was so focused on what others wanted me to do, thinking they had the answers for me, that when I finally found what I really wanted to do, I was blinded, and I couldn't see it until it was too late.

I lost the love of my life because I didn't choose for myself.

I'm not saying that your life should revolve around partners (Please.) But keep close to the people that make life feel more fun, the ones that keep your mind from thinking about the what ifs. The ones who give you the best experiences.

I want my daughter to experience as much as she can for no reason other than just for fun. I experienced all that I did in high school as a way to "figure myself out" and I didn't really experience anything for fun until college. Now I know that figuring yourself out is overrated.

Don't be stubborn like me. Find the ones who guide you to your own path without even realizing they're doing so. Hold them tight. Never doubt yourself.

I love you truly, deeply, always.

I found the cutest blue flower and decided to press it and preserve it in a necklace. I plan to give it to you when you are older. For now, it is kept safely in the back of this notebook.

Charlie re-read that passage repeatedly. Her mother had been just like her, had been confused about what she wanted, and had answers from no one. It was then that Charlie realized that if she went seeking answers from others, she would find ones she didn't want. She would play a part that was not meant for her.

Her hands flipped through the rest of the journal making sure she hadn't missed any more passages. She got to the back of the journal, there she saw the small, hollow space that had been meticulously carved out from the back cover. The hollow was neat, with clean edges. Inside this secret compartment, nestled in a small display case, lay a blue flower that was delicately pressed and encased within a circular pendant. The flower's five petite, star-shaped blossoms were arranged with intricate precision, their soft blue hue contrasting beautifully with the surrounding gold.

Charlie carefully removed the display case from its compartment and lifted the lid. She held up the necklace by its gold chain and admired its appearance. The pendant was crafted from a clear, glass-like material that allowed the flower to be viewed from all angles. The edges of the pendant were framed in a thin, elegant gold frame that highlighted the flower's color.

Suspended from a refined, gold chain, the pendant swung gracefully with every movement. The chain itself was dainty but sturdy. Lily's love of pressed flowers and gold jewelry was reflected in this piece. Charlie held the necklace in her hand gently and re-read the passage one more time. She had felt closer to her mother than she had in a long time. A weight had been lifted off of her, her mother wouldn't be disappointed if she stayed here or decided to work at the library. She would be disappointed if she denied herself anything good.

This caused her to wonder if staying here really was good enough for her. She wasn't sure, but there was no use in trying to figure that out now. She would discover that as she went.

It was going to be hard to shake the fact that she shouldn't be worrying about the next steps in life, reprogramming her brain to understand that she did not have to have it all figured out. But while she had time left, she was going to enjoy the last few school years with her friends, she would try and make the most of college.

For the first time, Charlie May was going to attempt to go blindly into life without a plan.

Chapter 24

Forget Me Not

"Only three more days left of our break," Amelie said with a groan rolling onto her back "I'm not excited to go back to class."

"What, you don't like being bored to death in Mrs. Jones's math class?" Charlie joked from her spot on the floor next to her.

The three were hanging out in Oliver's basement, they had made up for what had happened at the edge of town the other day. Charlie had recounted Vivian's letter and some parts of her mother's journal. Mainly that she had no idea what she was doing either and was also figuring it out as she went.

Amelie stuck her tongue out before her eyes caught the new necklace swinging gently from around her friend's neck. "Cute necklace, where did you get it from?" she rolled on her stomach to get a better look.

"Oh, my mom made it," Charlie says looking down at it with a soft smile "It was in the journal in this little compartment thing, she wrote that she made it for me."

"A forget-me-not, very fitting," Oliver said with his head against Charlie's lap.

This did not faze Charlie. Oliver was very touchy when it came to people he was close with. Amelie resorted to hugs only for Charlie and maybe a high five for Oliver, and Charlie was only ever comfortable with Amelie and Oliver being in her space. "Why do you know so much about flowers? You knew all of the ones in my mom's memory box."

"My mom was a florist before she decided to be a stay-at-home mom," he said casually. "That is actually how she and my dad met. He was buying flowers for his mom after some kind of surgery."

"That's actually really cute Oliver," Amelie said sounding surprised.

"She liked to teach my brothers and I about the different kinds of flowers and what they mean," he continued "I was really the only one that it stuck with. We started a garden in our backyard." A small smile crept onto his face.

Amelie's expression softened and she glanced down at her hands "Oliver, I'm sorry that I assumed you didn't spend time with your mother. It wasn't right of me to say that just because you didn't know who her college friends were," she sighed softly "I think I was just jealous that your mom is around so much and available for commentary about her life, I just thought you were taking her for granted."

Oliver laughs softly "I never would," he sits up "Don't apologize Amelie, I'm sorry too. It wasn't nice of me to try and hurt you that way"

Amelie gave him a soft smile then paused for a moment "Can I ask you a question?"

"Shoot,"

"I can't fathom the idea of not giving all your ability to make sure you get into a good school and have some kind of image built up. Appearances were all that I was taught, how does it not bother you that you might just have a normal life?"

Oliver took a moment to ponder his answer. He never really thought about what others were thinking about him at any given moment. He had watched his older brother be the star of the school due to his athletics, that pressure had been handed to him by their father. It never interested Oliver to be something that others would look to. He just did things for himself, he was the only one that had to live with himself. "I don't have to be something great. I am Jamie and Noah's son. I'm pretty proud of that"

His words settled in the air for a moment before Amelie spoke up. "I got into Brightwater Academy. It's a college two hours away from here. It's perfect because it's in the same city as the main location where my internship is," she continued "My mom also graduated from there. So, you know she was excited that I got in."

"Good job, love," Charlie said with a soft smile. The pain of Amelie leaving didn't sting as bad. She was excited for her friend to go on this journey.

"Two hours isn't too far," Oliver pointed out "Are you planning on visiting?"

"Duh," Amelie laughed "You think I'm just going to forget about this place forever?"

"I want us to keep hanging out with each other" Charlie blurted out. She stared at the confused faces of her friends and started over "I mean I know we are going to keep hanging out, but I mean I want to go and do things we haven't done before, starting Senior year." Charlie knew this was going to sound odd coming from her, and she wasn't going to experiment all that much, but she would attempt to be more flexible "I-I might not always participate but I will try and work on not just sitting back to watch."

Amelie grins "So you'll stop pretending to be busy when we plan activities?"

"We can go bowling!" Oliver exclaimed.

"I will be willing to watch bowling," she says. Bowling was something she tried but did not enjoy participating in.

"Roller skating?" Amelie asked.

"Go Karts!" Oliver spoke.

"Karaoke night" Amelie suggested with a wide grin.

"Don't push your luck," Charlie said with a joking grin. She was terrified of trying new things and she would still abide by her own personal rules, but she was done closing herself off and wasting her high school years alone. She was lucky enough to have friends who would include her just by letting her hang out on the sidelines. They never made her feel bad about it or tried to get her to do something that made her uncomfortable.

"Ooh, I'll make a schedule for which activities we can do," Amelie says standing up "We are gonna make Senior year great! I'm going to get my notebook, I'll be back!" She says running up the stairs to grab her stuff where she left it when they all first got here.

Oliver looked over at Charlie and gave her a soft smile "You're nervous about roller skating, aren't you?"

Charlie chuckled lightly "How did you know?"

"You looked like you were about to call off the whole idea," He says with a small laugh "Don't worry, I'll teach you. Besides, watching Amelie shoulder check the skaters that don't follow the designated skating path, is way more fun to watch up close."

Charlie loved spending time with her friends, getting enjoyment from watching them experience the fun. It was fun enough for her. However, she couldn't stop thinking about her mom and how Jamie said that she was always doing something exciting. She wanted to try it, in her own way.

Chapter 25

80's Carpet & Fast-Food Fries

Senior Year

"First Period: Senior English Mrs. Williams, Second Period: AP Government Mr. Smith, then I have third and fourth period free. What about you guys?" Charlie and her friends were in her room comparing class schedules for school that started soon.

"First Period: Senior English with Williams, Second Period AP Government with Smith, I have third period free, but I have my internship study for fourth period." Amelie read. "Lifestyle Event Planning has a small branch here in town, so I'll be going there to get some hands-on experience."

Oliver read over his in his head before speaking "Senior English, Graphic Design 2, Government, and College Algebra" He paused "Charlie how did you get away with only having two classes?"

"I already took all the required classes besides the Senior level ones," She shrugs "I didn't want to take college algebra because I heard Mr. Daniels is the worst."

"It wasn't required?" He groaned "I'm not even gonna request to drop it, it'll just be one less class I have to take in college."

"Why didn't you take AP Government?" Amelie asked confused.

He huffs. "I don't even like learning about Government normally, there was no way I was going to be able to focus in that class. The real question is why in the world did you two take AP?"

"It looks good to have a lot of honors classes," Amelie says with a shrug "Charlie took all honors classes, or else she would be booored," the girl said, dragging out the word while gently shaking Charlie's shoulders.

Charlie laughed and pushed her away gently. It was true that Charlie took a lot of honors classes, and she enjoyed learning and thrived in the fast-paced learning environment. It was nice to be surrounded by people who made her think from a different point of view "Also, I'm pretty sure that not a lot of people take AP Government so the class size should be relatively small. That's always a bonus."

Oliver shook his head in mock disbelief. "I'm so humbly honored that you two didn't go to smart people, gifted high schools, and leave me alone with the peasants that don't want to be drowned in homework."

"You're welcome," Amelie replied.

Charlie thought that Oliver didn't give himself enough credit, he was plenty smart. She was about to say as much when she noticed his playful smile, realizing that he was probably just joking with them.

"Alright, who is ready for roller skating tonight!" Amelie says holding up her notebook, outlining the activities she had planned for their last year together.

"I'm ready to watch some people get absolutely demolished by this 5'11 chaos of destruction on wheels." Oliver grins rubbing his hands together.

Amelie tossed her braids over her shoulders. "What can I say, I do it for the fans."

"I'm surprised you haven't gotten kicked out yet for doing all that." Charlie giggled, secretly enjoying Amelie's extroverted, chaotic personality.

"People skate on the wrong side of the rink, they deserve to get checked. I'm pretty sure the employees are secretly rooting for me," She looked down at her notebook "Okay, I say we meet up at 7:30. I'm gonna be eating dinner at 5:30 cause my dad is cooking."

"I was just about to ask who was going to be in charge of feeding me," Oliver says standing up.

"You got to fend for yourself this time white boy," Amelie says standing up.

"Wow. Haven't heard that one since Freshman year," He extended his hand to Charlie and helped her up.

"Thought I'd bring it back for one more year." She turns her attention to Charlie "Do you need me to come pick you up?"

Charlie didn't have a car, Skylar convinced Aaron that she didn't need one because almost everything was within walking distance. She nodded softly "Yeah if you don't mind"

"You know I got you," Amelie said as if it was obvious.

It was obvious. Amelie had always taken care of Charlie. She stuck up for her in school, gave her rides when it wasn't convenient to walk, and came over to help babysit when it got overwhelming.

"Thanks" She walked the two to the door "I'll see you guys later"

Charlie was now sitting in the passenger seat of Amelie's car. The closer they got to the roller rink, the more nervous Charlie felt. She had never skated before, she usually sat and watched, maybe played some arcade games. She was so nervous that she had researched what the best attire was for roller skating. She wore a dark green tank top and black high-waisted leggings, she had spent a good minute trying to find the best pair of socks that wouldn't slip down while she was skating.

Soon Amelie pulled into the parking lot, Charlie looked out the window at the neon purple lights that wrapped around the roof of the building. Once the car was parked the girls got out and headed inside the double doors.

Charlie was immediately hit with a mixture of popcorn and B.O., loud music and the sounds of people talking, and arcade music. Thankfully they hadn't started the strobe lights sequence yet. She hated that. They walked along the blue carpet that had color full shape designs that reminded Charlie of the 80s.

Charlie spotted Oliver first, leaning against the counter watching the skaters on the rink in front of him. He turned, met Charlie's eyes, and smiled softly "Guys! I wasn't late for once!"

"Wow, I guess there is hope for you after all," Amelie joked making her way to him.

"Awe, but my favorite quote was you saying that a lot of things were changing this year but you being late was not one of them" Charlie fake pouted.

Oliver cackled at the memory "A lot of things have changed this year but me being on time is not one of them" He quoted himself "I can't believe you remembered that!"

"Well yeah, we were waiting for you for about an hour. It was almost a new record" Charlie said while giggling.

Oliver grinned and pushed off the counter as a lady from behind the counter came back with his skates "Well I already got us paid for" He grabbed his skates "I'll see you guys over on the bench" He walked off to go sit and change his shoes.

Amelie turned to the lady at the counter "A size eight and a size six please" she spoke politely and watched the woman disappear to the back, returning shortly handing the girls their shoes.

Charlie took hers and followed Amelie to where Oliver had been sitting waiting. She took off her shoes and put them next to Oliver's and Amelie's. She laced up her skates and slowly stood up.

"I'll see you out there!" Amelie hollers, skating out to the rink.

The roller-skating rink buzzed with activity, colorful lights reflecting off the polished wooden floor as skaters glided around the track. The upbeat music pulsed through the air, and the atmosphere of it all made Charlie's nerves rise.

Charlie, her face flushed with a mix of anticipation and uncertainty, stood near the edge of the rink. She worried that her skates were far too large for her feet even though she had known her size, their bright neon wheels standing out starkly against the dark blue carpet. Oliver stood beside her, offering a reassuring smile.

"You ready?" Oliver asked, noticing Charlie's apprehension.

Charlie nodded, though her eyes betrayed her nervousness. "I think so. I just… I'm not sure I'm going to be very good at this."

Oliver chuckled softly. "You probably won't be, I know I wasn't. We will take it slow, and I'll guide you."

He extended a steady hand, and Charlie took it gratefully. As they approached the rink's entrance, Oliver gave her a few pointers. "Keep your knees slightly bent and your weight centered. It's all about balance."

Charlie tried to focus on his instructions, her heart racing as she took her first tentative steps onto the rink. The wheels wobbled beneath her, and she felt an unsettling lurch in her stomach. Oliver's hand was firm and comforting, and he guided her along slowly.

"See? Not so bad," Oliver said, his voice encouraging. "Just keep your movements smooth. It's like walking, but with wheels."

Charlie took a deep breath, biting back a sarcastic comment, and attempted to mimic his movements. She took a few more steps, her arms flailing slightly for balance. Oliver stayed close.

"You're doing great," he said. "Try to relax. The more you tense up, the harder it is."

Charlie bit her lip, trying to follow his advice. The initial fear of falling was still there, but with each step, she gained a bit more confidence. Oliver's patience and gentle guidance made a world of difference.

"Now, let's try gliding a bit," Oliver suggested. "Push off with one foot and then the other."

Charlie hesitated for a moment before following his instructions. She pushed off with one foot and then the other, her movements awkward but gradually smoother. Oliver's hand remained firmly in hers, and his encouraging words helped her keep her focus.

"I'm actually doing it!" Charlie exclaimed, a mix of surprise and excitement in her voice.

Oliver grinned, giving her a supportive squeeze. "You're doing awesome! Better than sitting on the sidelines?"

As they skated around the rink together, Charlie's fear started to fade, replaced by a growing sense of exhilaration. The music seemed to pulse with her newfound rhythm, and she found herself laughing as she started to get the hang of it. This feeling is what she had been missing out on this whole time?

"Thank you for being so patient," Charlie said, her face bright with a genuine smile. "I didn't think I'd get the hang of it this quickly."

Oliver's smile never left his face. "You have to give yourself a bit more credit Charlie."

Charlie nodded, feeling the warmth of his encouragement. As they continued to skate, her confidence grew with each lap, and the rink's vibrant energy matched the joy she felt.

Amelie caught back up with Charlie, and Oliver "Look at you Char!" She says excitedly "You're gonna be checking people in no time"

Charlie laughed as the three skated together under the glittering lights of the rink. The upbeat music pulsed through the air, and their wheels clicked rhythmically against the floor as they glided effortlessly in sync. Amelie twirled gracefully, her laughter mingling with the music, while Charlie and Oliver skated close, sharing jokes and playful jabs. The joy of the vibrant atmosphere and the infectious beat made every turn and spin a celebration.

Charlie felt so immersed in the moment she was almost sadden when she heard the music get lowered and the announcer coming over the loudspeaker. The lights dimmed slightly as the voice spoke "Attention skaters! It's time for a slow skate. Please reduce your speed and enjoy the mellow tunes." The upbeat melody faded, replaced by a smooth, soothing track. The rink's atmosphere shifted to a more serene vibe, with skaters gradually slowing down.

Amelie looks back at her group and grins wildly "Someone over there caught my attention, Gonna shoot my shot" She saluted the others and skated off.

"Oh, that girl is something else" Charlie murmured softly.

"Don't worry, I'm not going anywhere" Oliver teased her.

The vibrant lights dimming to create a more intimate atmosphere. The once energetic skaters now moved gracefully. Oliver and Charlie skated side by side, their movements synchronized in a soothing rhythm.

Oliver's hand brushed against Charlie's as they skated, his fingers lingering just enough to be a gentle touch. He noticed how she seemed to relax in the peaceful, almost dreamy ambiance that enveloped them.

"Slow down a bit," Oliver said, his voice gentle as he guided her with a reassuring hand on her back. "It's nice to just take it all in."

Charlie looked at him with a small smile, her eyes soft and reflective. "You know, I've come to realize that sometimes I'm not here" She started "Like I live inside myself. But sometimes I'll see something so beautiful that I can see clearly through the haze and am overcome with the sensation of being human" She paused, looked around then looked back at him "This is beautiful"

Oliver's heart skipped a beat at her words. He glanced at her, noticing the way her eyes seemed to sparkle under the soft lights, how her voice had mellowed into a serene tone. The slow pace of their skating gave him the chance to savor each moment, each subtle shift in her expression.

As they moved around the rink, Oliver stole glances at Charlie. He admired the way she seemed to lose herself in the music, her gaze occasionally drifting toward him with a contented look. He could feel the warmth of her presence, the way she fit naturally into the space beside him, and it made his pulse quicken.

Charlie, absorbed in the gentle sway of the music, was unaware of the quiet tension between them. She was simply enjoying the moment, the calm after the earlier excitement. She glanced at Oliver but had not picked up on the way he looked at her.

"This is really nice, Oliver," she said, her voice low and sincere. "Thanks for being there for me no matter the pace."

Oliver's eyes softened, and he nodded, his smile tender. "Always, Charlie."

As they continued to glide around the rink, Oliver admired her more deeply than he had before, and the slow skate was a moment of quiet revelation for him. He longed to tell her how he felt, his mother's words whispering in his ear, but for now, he was content to cherish these simple, intimate moments.

The two had always been on different paths but Oliver was ready to walk with her as long as it took. Taking what he could from the shared moments, the quiet, beautiful connection that was as slow and sweet as the music that surrounded them.

The three decided to stop skating and spent the last thirty minutes playing the arcade games. Amelie was kicking Oliver's butt at basketball while telling Charlie about the number she had gotten. "I'm about to win a second time tonight," she said before shooting one more point than Oliver before the buzzer went off.

When it was time to part, Amelie claimed she wanted to get home before her mom did, so she didn't wake her up.

"I thought your mom didn't work today?" Oliver asked, confused.

Amelie shot him a look "I don't know what you're talking about Oliver, my mom has work tonight"

"But I thought your dad was-"

"Oliver." Amelie cut in "Take Charlie home" she said through gritted teeth. She turned her attention to Charlie and hugged her "I had so much fun, I'm glad you decided to do this."

"Me too. Text me when you get home" she says hugging her back.

"Will do. I Love you!" Amelie waved and walked off to her car.

"Love you too" Charlie replied watching her get in her car before following Oliver to his car.

"Is it bad that I'm kind of hungry?" He laughed jogging over to open the passenger door for her.

Charlie chuckled "I really want some fries" She got in the car and buckled in.

"You read my mind" he shut her door and got in on the driver's side. He buckled in and started to drive to the nearest fast-food restaurant.

Now the two were parked in the almost empty parking lot of the restaurant as there wasn't much else to do. Both of them enjoying their fries and sodas.

"I am not ready for school to start back up" Charlie said after a moment.

"Really? I'd be ecstatic if I only had two classes"

"Well, I'm not worried about the classes, I just don't like the awkward ice breakers and having to talk with the people I don't know in class"

"Yeah, those icebreakers are pointless" He said with a small laugh "Well for Government you said there weren't a lot of kids in that class, and you have Amelie there. And Senior English is all Seniors, so you'll have both of us"

Charlie thought about it for a moment, glad that she had her last two Senior classes with her friends. "I'm not ready to talk about fun facts in the ice breakers. I don't have a fun fact about myself" she takes a drink "and I'm going to be hearing more about colleges and" she sighs "It's scary"

"If you think about it, no one's fun fact is actually fun. It's a lot of kids bragging about their vacations or something" he shrugs "I'm just going to talk about the garden me and my mom have. That seems to satisfy them"

Charlie blinked "A fun fact about you doesn't have to be something like actually cool?"

He shakes his head "It's more of a talking point. You could really say whatever you want, there isn't a guideline for these kinds of things"

Charlie groaned and closed her eyes laying her head back against the head rest earning a laugh from Oliver. "Sometimes I really don't understand people"

He turns to face her "We can practice, what would you make your fun fact be?"

Charlie turns to look at him, she was usually so skilled at avoiding direct eye contact but found herself caught in a rare moment of vulnerability. His gaze held a gentle encouragement as if he was silently telling her that whatever she had to say was worth the wait.

The usual walls she kept up were momentarily lowered, revealing a more earnest and contemplative side as she eventually convinced herself to speak. "I think I would talk about my mom" She spoke softly, her hand gently reaching for her necklace "How she liked to press flowers, and that she made me this necklace"

"I think that's a perfect fun fact Charlie" Oliver said, his voice gentle. "Your fun fact already beat everyone else fun facts" That earned a laugh that he enjoyed hearing so much.

"I think your fun fact is a good one too," Charlie tells him "You get to have a fun hobby with your mom, and you get to share your knowledge on flowers"

He chuckled "I think you might be the only one interested in hearing flowers and their meanings. Well, you and Vivian" He nodded "She likes when things have meaning too. I was over at her house one day and continued noticing how many blue items were there. I figured it was her favorite color and asked why."

"It's because Dezi Carter saw her as wise and intelligent" Charlie finished thinking back to the letter.

"Yeah. Vivian said she used it as a reminder that she's not stuck here, the answer for her life is only something she can figure out" he looks at her "That's why I wasn't surprised when you told us her reasoning for giving you the acorn. Viv likes symbols."

Charlie thought about it for a moment, thinking about how Amelie had accepted the fact that she wasn't going to be the one to solve this problem. Her mother's life wasn't going to be the answer to Charlie's life now. "Yeah, sounds like I'm going to be solving my curse problem on my own"

Oliver looks over at her confused "What? You don't have to figure out it alone"

"Well, I'm the reason I'm stuck here, no passion to leave or whatever" She started waving her hand slightly "I lost Ms. Vivian and her wise words to answer any questions I had. I thought learning about my mother could help me figure out what I want with my life. And even Amelie thought she could solve it by getting me to find a career or forming an interest in finding Grayson. She told me that she couldn't be able to solve this for me"

Oliver was quiet for a moment before nodding slowly "Sure we can't tell you what to do with your life, because if we're being honest that wouldn't give you any kind of motivation. But we can still be there for you. We're always going to help you in whatever way we can, in whatever way you want"

Charlie hadn't thought about it like that, she just assumed that after Amelie gave up and her mother's stories were a dead end. She figured her friends would move on and she would be left alone. It didn't occur to her that they would still stick around "Why have you never asked what I wanted to do after college?"

Oliver raised his eyebrow "Why would I?" he asked curiously.

"Everyone does?" she says confused "Its right up at the top of the list. Name, Age, what do you want to do with your life?"

Oliver chuckled in agreement "Fair. However, I am not interested in what people want to do for a living, which often doesn't match up with what they dream of" He says softly "You learn a lot from what drives people"

"What is it you dream of?" she asked, not having a clue what hers was.

Oliver's eyes met her for a moment, taking in every detail of her face. All he wanted right now was to be back at that skating rink with Charlie, in that moment where it felt like it was just them. He grinned slightly. "Right now? Surviving high school"

Chapter 26

Pretty Not Fragile

Knight Household

Oliver pulled into his driveway after dropping Charlie off. They had spent an hour together in the parking lot just talking, before she had realized the time and wanted to get home before everyone in her house went to bed. Oliver had dropped her off and made sure she got inside safely.

He walked inside, shutting the door behind him but didn't move. The moment at the roller rink played over in his head, he couldn't get the image of Charlie's smiling face out of his head, the way she seemed to glow in the lights of the rink. She had glided so effortlessly against the floor as if she was a natural.

"Someone's thinking pretty hard over here" A soft voice said shaking him from his daydream.

Oliver looked over and saw his mother on the couch with a book in her lap. He didn't know how he hadn't realized her sitting there, illuminated by the table lamp. He groans and flops down on the couch, inching his way up to lay his head on his mother's lap.

Jamie laughed softly and moved the book away so he could lie more comfortably. Her hand ran gently through his hair. "I know, kid"

He shakes his head "She's so pretty" he whispers.

Jamie was slightly amused by how enamored her son was over his best friend "Well have you told her?"

Oliver sat up and looked at his mother with wide eyes. "No!" he then hesitated before shaking his head "I couldn't"

"Why not?"

He was quiet for a moment contemplating how to put these thoughts into the right words. "She's been through a lot. I don't want to overwhelm her"

"She's not fragile Ollie" She reminds him.

"Oh, I know" The memory of Charlie using the forcefield as a punching bag came to mind.

Jamie looks at him "I know you will figure it all out Oliver. I can't give you the answers" She stands up "Get some sleep, you need to fix your sleep schedule"

Oliver waved to his mother and laid back down on the couch staring at the ceiling. He didn't want to waste time sitting on his feelings about her, but he didn't want to scare her off. He wanted to be there to help her not just break this curse, but also enjoy life.

She had seemed to like roller skating tonight, he had hoped that tonight had been fun enough for her to want to keep trying new things. He was glad she seemed to be feeling better after the event at the end of town. Charlie seemed really hurt and he felt bad for not being able to do much to help her. He couldn't have helped her then, but he promised he would help her enjoy her Senior year before Amelie left. He knew neither girl was looking forward to graduation.

Chapter 27

Moments with Ms. Vivian

"You need a hobby kid" Vivian says watching Charlie sweep the hardwood floors of her living room. She had tried to keep her from doing any chores, but Charlie was a stubborn one "Why would anyone want to spend time with an old woman?"

"First off, I like spending time with you" Charlie scoffed "Secondly, I don't have a hobby" She paused when Vivian cleared her throat "Right, sorry. I haven't had a moment of free time to figure out a hobby" The girl corrected putting away the broom after sweeping the contents into the trashcan.

"Well, you like to read. That is a hobby" Vivian pointed out.

Charlie shrugs "But it isn't enough."

"What does that even mean?"

"I'm not doing anything useful with that. It's not like I'm creating something to sell or anything I can show off"

Vivian stared at her confused "That is not the point of a hobby" She tells her "What else do you like to do? Something you like, that's just purely for you and not used as an excuse to work"

Charlie was quiet for a moment, looking around the room to see if there was anything that would remind her of a past time that she liked to participate in. There were bookshelves lined with books, boxes of puzzles on the table, and balls of yarn on the chair. None of these things, besides reading, had ever given her any interest. She wasn't a fan of puzzles, but she tried once, looking down at the jumbled messed stressed her out as she wasn't sure where to start.

She had tried to learn to crochet from Ms. Vivian but when she had gone home and worked on it, it seemed as if she had forgotten everything she had ever learned. It was so stressful, she was smart, and she knew she was smart. Papers and tests saved in a folder documented how smart she was. So, it felt so much more heartbreaking when she couldn't figure out something simple.

What else in her life had been something she had done purely for her own reasoning? She started working at the library because Amelie wanted to and some test told her to, she liked green because she was told it looked good on her. Charlie could not think of one single part of herself that she had figured out on her own "I guess I like a lot of things because of other people" She said slowly "Sometimes that worries me, is there something I like purely for me? I feel like an amalgamation of all the people in my life."

Vivian seemed satisfied with that answer, a small smile played on her lips "Isn't that wonderful?"

Chapter 28

Home

It was dark and it was quiet. Charlie felt like she wasn't herself, she felt very out of control of whatever was about to come before her. Slowly, the scene laid out in front of her, Amelie and Oliver stood in the woods staring at something that Charlie could not quite make out yet.

"I never understood you, you hate new things and change but you don't have any plan in place?!" Amelie shouted. Her voice sounded echoey and far away.

Before Charlie could make any movement, the rest of the scene started to play out. She saw herself pushing hard against the forcefield that kept her in her small town.

She was dreaming. All her dreams were like this, like she was watching things play out like a movie, much like life, Charlie rarely felt like she was seeing her own life through her own eyes.

"Why don't you want to get out of here!" Dream Amelie shouted again.

Charlie continued to watch herself struggle to meet her friends on the other side. She wanted to wake up, but a part of her felt like she needed to relive this moment again.

She looked back over at Amelie whose face now seemed dark and cold "You are either forced to follow in your parent's footsteps or disappoint them. Or you forget who you are as a person."

Charlie had had enough and forced herself awake, now sitting upright in her bed, her breathing heavy as she looked around trying to ground herself. She was awake now, that was just a dream, she and Amelie had made up.

The girl laid back down in her bed, staring at her ceiling. It just now hit her how badly Amelie's words had hurt her. Sure, she apologized, and Charlie accepted but she couldn't shake what it had meant to her.

Did Amelie not think that Charlie was angry about this situation? About being stuck here? Of course she was! She was going to miss her friends, she was upset, she had no plan and no real sense of self but that wasn't her fault. She didn't have a choice. After her mother's accident and she moved in with Aaron and Skylar, Charlie's life changed, she felt like she got reprogrammed. She was put to work taking care of her cousins and the house she lived in, anything to appease Skylar out of fear of stressing out Aaron who lost his sister and had never asked to take on the work of another kid, the fear of being kicked out with nowhere to go.

It was hard to remember the girl Charlie used to be, with her mother. She remembered vaguely, but it played out foggy and confusing, like a worn-out videotape. She knew she used to be more "fun", she remembered being friends with lots of people, not being afraid of putting herself out there, she laughed a lot more and didn't care what other people thought. She remembered some people who tried to make her care what they thought, the wrong friend group she briefly hung out with in middle school, the mean girl who told her humor was weird because she laughed at the most stupid things.

Charlie hadn't known why that had been such a bad thing, she liked being able to laugh at almost anything, to find anything funny. After a while Charlie realized those girls were no good for her so she stopped hanging out with them, of course, she always had Amelie and Oliver, but young Charlie liked to venture out and be friends with anyone she could.

Charlie remembered the moments she had with her mother, those memories she could recall seeing from her own point of view. One moment often replayed in her dreams, leaving Charlie a feeling bittersweet when she woke up.

Lily had come home with two paint cans in her hand. Charlie had been laying on the living room floor reading a book she had gotten from Ms. Vivian a few days before.

"What's that for?" Young Charlie asked curiously, closing her book.

"I think it's time to redecorate this room," Lily says setting the cans down on the floor "Want to help?"

Lily didn't wait for Charlie's response as she started to move the couch and the tables to the middle of the room. Charlie stayed out of the way then went to help her mother lay out a tarp.

"You know what the best part of painting a room is?" Lily asked curiously while popping open the paint can.

Charlie tilted her head and shrugs "What?"

"You can draw anything you want on these walls, and they'll be hidden from everyone and only we'll know about it" She grins dipping her paint brush into the can before painting a smiley face on the wall in the blue paint.

Charlie watched her mother and giggled softly before picking up her own brush, dipping it into the paint as well. She looked at the wall for a moment before deciding to paint a heart.

The two of them spent a while just painting whatever they felt like on the walls. Charlie remembered a lot of laughter and dancing. They finished their artwork with a flower garden and Lily added a date. Charlie's birthday.

Charlie remembered they covered up their work but still had the memories of putting it there. It was something Charlie thought about every time she was in the living room, how her mother turned an ordinary task into something fun and memorable. Her mother had a gift for that.

Their home was always so warm and safe, every dinner Lily made was Charlie's favorite. Her mother just made everything make sense, without her, Charlie felt so lost.

Charlie sat up in her bed and felt a longing in her chest again. She wanted her mother, she wanted everything to make sense. She wanted to go home.

Quietly, Charlie climbed out of bed and moved across the room to flip on her bedroom light. It took a moment for her eyes to adjust but once she could see, she wasted no time slipping on her socks and shoes and grabbing her sweatshirt from her closet. Before she left her bedroom, she turned off her light and slipped downstairs.

She moved quietly down the stairs, through the living room and to the door. Holding her breath, she opened the door and went outside.

The cold air hit her face, shocking her system, but she didn't let that slow her down. She took off fast back to her old street. She ran past the park and the diner and finally came to her old street. She slowed down when she noticed the pale-yellow house before her, she took a moment to take in thc sight of the place she used to call home. She wanted to go up to the porch, turn the doorknob and go inside. She wanted to relive all her favorite memories. Her feet dragged her to the porch, but she stopped seeing that she was not alone.

Chapter 29

A Pale-Yellow House Frozen In Time

Amelie had been sitting in her desk chair staring at her laptop screen. It was almost midnight, and she hadn't been able to sleep so she decided to get a head start on her homework. However, she had only gotten halfway through her AP Gov homework before her mind started to trail off. She thought about how much fun she had at the roller rink with Charlie and Oliver. It had felt like things had been so stressful since they discovered Charlie was cursed, that tonight was a good break from all the stress.

She'd had fun, and she knew Charlie had fun too. She had seen how happy she had looked while skating with Oliver. Amelie wasn't dumb, she knew Oliver had a crush on Charlie, she called it back their Sophomore year and teased him about it but promised to keep it a secret because it wasn't hers to tell. She trusted Oliver, he was a good guy who cared about Charlie just as much Amelie had.

She knew Oliver made Charlie happy, that he could help her when Amelie couldn't. She was just happy to see Charlie being put first, she always took care of everyone, put everyone first, and all Amelie wanted for her friend was to have someone who took care of her for once.

Amelie thought about her friendship with Charlie and how she had started to be a bit distant since Junior year. Amelie had been told by her mother to focus more on school and less with her friends, and

Charlie was so focused helping her aunt and uncle that the two didn't spend as much time as they usually did.

Amelie felt terrible for not always being there for Charlie like she had used to. When Junior year was over the group's schedule had finally aligned and they had been able to spend more consistent time with each other. Once they learned about Charlie's curse, it shattered Amelie. She didn't want Charlie to be here alone, didn't like that Charlie felt confused about what she wanted out of her life. Amelie still felt so terrible for snapping at her, she had just wanted to help Charlie but realized she had gone about it the wrong way.

Instead of trying to make Charlie happy the way that worked for Amelie, she would try and make Charlie happy in a way that worked for Charlie. To Amelie, that now meant making Grand Fayword memorable for her best friend once college started. She wanted Charlie to be okay after she left for college. She knew graduation was going to suck, she didn't want to be away from her friend, but she would feel a little better if she knew her friend was taken care of.

She was going to do her best to make Charlie's Senior year a blast, no expectations of breaking the curse, just good moments.

"Oliver was good at making Charlie happy." Amelie thought. The two had grown a bit closer while Amelie had been distanced for school, they had their own inside jokes, and he made her laugh like Amelie hadn't seen Charlie do in a while.

She thought about how happy Charlie used to be before the accident. She thought about how Jamie Knight had stepped in a lot during the hard times when Charlie needed a mother figure. It made Amelie slightly bitter that her own mother couldn't be the one to help, not that it should've surprised her, Angela Henderson was barely good at being there for her own kid.

Amelie missed Lily May a lot.

Before she knew it, Amelie was walking down the quiet lamplit street. She was thankful she remembered her coat as the cold wind whipped in her face. This was utterly stupid but felt like it was something she needed to do.

She looked up at the street sign **Oak** and turned down onto it, there at the end of the street sat a small pale-yellow house, the wood porch looked brand new, probably due to the town's upkeep for it. Her eyes trailed over to the mailbox head that rested carefully on the porch, hand painted flowers highlighted the last name that was also hand painted

May

Amelie stood in front of her friend's old house taking in the scene before her. The outside of the house was so well taken care of that for a moment one might believe that someone lived there, but that house had never been sold. No one ever bought it, for whatever reason, but some of the people in town always came by to fix up the porch when the wood started to rot away, someone had saved the mailbox head and kept it on the porch to keep the weather from fading it.

She knew she had no reason to feel this sad. This was not her mother, her mother was alive and well. Only Charlie should be feeling this way, Amelie had no reason to miss Lily like this. But she did. Amelie grew up spending so much time at Lily's house with Charlie that Lily took care of her like a mother should have.

"Weird how the renovations make this place seem frozen in time" A voice from behind startled Amelie. She turned and saw Charlie standing behind her, making her way into the yard. Her hair was pulled up into a bun on the top of her head, she too was bundled in her sweatshirt.

Amelie nodded softly and looked back at the house "I am so sorry Charlie" she said softly. "For what I did back there that day. I know I already apologized but I can't shake how guilty I feel for hurting you like that. Like how my mother hurts me"

Charlie stared up at the house and didn't say anything.

"I shouldn't be here feeling sad like this. I wasn't the one who was hurt" she continued.

"Why are you here?"

Amelie looked at her and blinked "What?" When Charlie didn't answer Amelie stayed quiet and thought hard about it. "I don't know I guess I was just thinking about my mom… then about yours" she says quietly. "Your mom was much more present in my life than mine ever was. Much prouder of me" She whispers. "And I'm not in any way saying that qualifies me to know exactly what you are feeling. But it makes me feel like such a crappy person."

"My mother's death makes you feel like a crappy person?" Charlie turned her head.

"No! No," Amelie stuttered out. "Not that. It's just" She thought about it for a moment "I always felt kind of jealous when your mother praised all your accomplishments and went to all your events. She was proud of you" She shoved her hands in the pockets of her jacket and continued "Hell she was even proud of my accomplishments, she started to become the first person I wanted to tell"

Amelie turns and looks at Charlie noticing the confused look on the girl's face. She knew that Charlie was trying to be there for her, so she could do her best to get the jumbled mess of thoughts into words. "But Angela is still my mother, and it is wrong of me to mourn when my mother is still alive"

She couldn't look at her friend's face anymore, now turning to look back at the house "Then I just get so angry when I compare my mother and yours, because I know that if anyone treated me the way Angela Henderson treated me, I would drop them." She chewed on her lip "I hate that I feel so guilty for loving my mother even when she's hurt me. I don't know why I do it"

"Amelie she is your mother." Charlie started, "No one else in the world could be like that. It's biology, a tricky thing, a mother and child relationship"

Hearing her name made her flinch like she was about to be in trouble for expressing what had been weighing on her. But that never came.

"Your mother is a complex person. That's just what people are" She continued softly "She can do bad things and still have good moments and vice versa. You aren't wrong for loving her"

Amelie looked down at the ground and kicked at the dirt refusing to let herself cry. "I don't know why she does this to me. I love her so much, why do I keep trying so hard to get her to love me back"

Charlie stared at her friend for a moment, her head tilting as she tried to figure her out. "You're still just a kid" She says simply "It's complex. Do you think you could adjust to the idea that your mom is a person and the things she does is not a direct result of something you've done?"

Amelie sat with that and thought for a moment "I've never let myself really sit with how I'm feeling, I usually just let it go and forget about it" She mumbled "I always got in trouble for feeling… anything really" she takes a deep breath and slowly sat down in the grass, the weight of realization being too much for her to continue standing. "I want to be able to love my mother without feeling bad about it. I think it'll take time for me to think of it in a way that she isn't directly a bad person. That I'm not a bad person for loving her, without it taking a big toll on me" She looked up at the house "I will figure out a way to come to terms with the fact that, yeah my mom sucks sometimes, but I can still love her and not have it hurt"

Charlie sat down with her and kept her eyes on the house in front of her "You don't need to figure it all out right now. Just sit with it for a moment, exist."

Amelie laughs softly "Good because this whole situation feels like a giant tangled ball of yarn" She leans her head on Charlie's shoulder "It's too much for tonight"

"I'll be here as long as it takes to untangle it"

Amelie stayed quiet for a moment processing all the feelings flowing through her. She could feel tears forming in her eyes, but she knew she wouldn't be able to let them go. Trying to cope with the fact that she couldn't write off her mom as a bad person, that she still loved her despite it all, was confusing. It was not what she expected when she came down here tonight.

She wasn't exactly sure what she was expecting when she came here.

"You know, I think it's pretty funny that we were both thinking about my mom so much that we decided to come to visit the house," Charlie said with a small laugh "I was thinking about the time she decided to redecorate the whole living room, just on a whim"

Amelie laughs with her "I remember that. I walked into your house and the living room walls were a deep, dark blue, even though they were just brown the other day when I was there" The girl stretched out her legs and chuckled softly "I remember one time she brought you your lunch at school when you forgot it. She showed up with an extra container of stew for me. I remember thinking that it was such a motherly act."

Charlie chuckled softly and kept her eyes on the porch "Why is that?"

Amelie shrugs "Well you know my parents always worked late so I either ate alone or at friends' houses. And when they were home my dad was always the one cooking dinner." She takes a deep breath "And when your mother brought me lunch, such a small act of kindness, I mean, Lily was always doing things for me. She was the one to teach me how to braid my hair. She had shown me more compassion than my mother had ever shown me. This woman who wasn't my mother went out of her way to do something nice for me."

Angela was all she had.

Chapter 30

You Love Her Too

Charlie sat at the kitchen table with her laptop doing her reading assignment for AP Gov, she would have been done reading by now, but she had to stop every now and then to keep track of her youngest cousin, Austin.

Austin was three and a very hyperactive child, he liked to be doing what everyone else was doing. At first, Charlie tried to sit with him in her lap, but he soon got bored of sitting still and resorted to smacking the keys on her keyboard.

After that Charlie set him in his own chair, got him juice and a snack, and his toy laptop. "You're doing homework just like me, isn't that fun Austin" She hums sitting back in her spot.

Austin was pretty satisfied with that and kept himself busy. That was until he saw his father walk in, he squealed and reached for him excitedly.

"Hey baby," Aaron said swooping up the child. "What are you doing in here?" He asked confused.

"Oh, I was watching him," Charlie said, her eyes not leaving the laptop.

"Aren't you doing homework?" He asked confused, frowning when his niece nodded her head "Where is Skylar?"

"Went to the store with Victor" She replied.

Aaron sighed "I told her to stop making you watch the kids especially when you're busy" He sat down in the chair with Austin in his lap "You could've come and got me"

"She told me you were busy" She shrugged and continued her work. The two fell into a comfortable silence, Charlie typing away on her real keyboard and Austin on his fake one.

Charlie glanced over at Aaron and watched him play with Austin, teaching him how to play the mini game that was on the laptop, guessing the animal that made that sound.

"Aaron when you were my age, was it hard to decide your career path?"

Her uncle turned to her "What do you mean?"

"I've just been thinking a lot about what I want to do, and it's frustrating. People just keep saying that we're almost adults and we should have this all figured out, and so I assumed that when I got this far, I would have an easier time making these kinds of decisions." She takes a deep breath. "So did you always kind of want to be a supervisor at the grocery store?"

She wanted to assume that surely that was not what he expected for himself, but she didn't want to be rude if it was true.

Aaron thought for a moment and sighed "Well, running the family business was something I did grow to like, I didn't want to be in charge of my own store, but I did like the managing aspect" He paused for a moment "So I guess in a way I did"

He noticed her face seem to fall, he hesitated for a moment before continuing "I never really considered pursuing my creative outlets as a career. However, just because I don't do them for work doesn't mean I didn't find time for them in life. I didn't give them up"

Charlie looked up at him and thought about that for a moment. She had remembered hearing Aaron talk about fixing up 'the old car in the garage' but she never realized that was something he found as a hobby. It kind of saddened her that she didn't know her uncle as well as she thought she did. "So, it's possible to have two things at once? A good career without giving up what you enjoy?"

Aaron nodded "Yes Charlie, I want you to understand that" He tells her "I didn't learn that until I got older, I thought you had to have one or the other" He got quiet for a moment, wondering how things might've been different if he knew then what he knew now.

"How did you get into fixing up cars?" She asked.

"Why? You interested in working with me?" He jokingly asked her

Charlie shrugs "I'm just curious how you stumbled upon it." She was secretly hoping for some advice, some kind of hobby she could have to help her balance out her life, to keep her from throwing herself into work.

He laughs softly "I think it was just something I did with my father" he says bouncing the baby in his lap "We always worked on cars on Sunday's when the store was closed. I kept it going because I liked it"

Charlie nodded softly even though that didn't help her. She didn't really have a tradition with her mother that's she could turn into a hobby. "Thanks Aaron" she says softly.

"You're welcome kid" He stood up with the baby and cleaned up his mess. "I'll talk to Skylar again about not bothering you when you're doing homework" he said before walking out of the room.

The three kids were hanging out in Oliver's basement. Amelie was working on her homework while Oliver and Charlie made a game of shooting hair ties at each other. It was Friday night, their typical get together movie night.

"You almost done yet Ame?" Charlie asked before shooting the band at Oliver.

"Almost," Amelie mumbled "I hate this stupid essay and this stupid book"

"I liked it," Oliver says picking up the band that landed by his feet "I thought it was kind of sweet."

"Sweet?" Amelie scoffs "What's sweet about some girl feeling like a backup plan just because all her friends are being chosen for sports and plays and stuff." Her finger continued typing away on her laptop. "Then only feeling like she belongs when some guy shows up. She never gave herself a fighting chance."

"Valid" Oliver started. "However, the main character just wants to know what it's like to be chosen, not just in relationships, but with friendships and sports and family. When the other character showed up, she learned that being chosen isn't about validation but embracing her own worth." He flicks the hair tie back at Charlie before standing up. "That's just what I wrote about. I gotta get my phone, I'll be back"

Charlie watched Oliver disappear before looking back at Amelie who had stopped typing and was now staring at her screen, chewing on her lip rather hard. "You okay Ame?"

"I did not write about that at all. I don't understand anything I have been writing" She laid her head down, burying her face in her arms.

This threw Charlie off a bit as Amelie was smart and always seemed on top of things, so for her to seem so discouraged over something like an English essay was strange. Charlie wasn't sure what to say so she asked again "You okay Ame?"

The girl was quiet for a moment before lifting her head slight, just barely making eye contact with her best friend "I just have so much going on. I just feel like" Her words fell out of her mouth slowly, but that still did not give her enough time to formulate an answer for how she was feeling.

Charlie's eyes scanned over her face, stopping at her tired eyes. "Like you're drowning?"

Amelie seemed a bit surprised, but that expression quickly faded back to her normal resting position. "Yes. It feels like I'm drowning but what's new." She lifted her head up and looked back at her laptop screen. "I am good at what I do. Drowning so beautifully that no one questions it."

That last part was barely audible, but Charlie heard it, she kept her eyes on Amelie as she tried to think of a solution. What would Amelie do if she was in this situation?

Oliver came flying down the stairs, jumping down the last few steps. "I'm back. Movie time?"

"Actually, it's nice out. Why don't we go to the park?" Charlie asked casually while she stood up and picked up her phone.

Amelie's brows furrowed slightly, eyes narrowing slightly "It's 9:30 Charlie."

Charlie just shrugged, tugging on her blue sweatshirt which she took off when she had arrived. Oliver's house was always warm, so she was just fine in her green T-shirt inside. "And? It's not like tomorrow is a school night or anything."

Amelie was at a loss for words, looking at Oliver for some kind of explanation.

"Hell yeah!" Oliver was already pulling his green hoodie over his head "That essay isn't due until next Tuesday Amelie, let's go!" He took off back upstairs.

Amelie stood up and slowly grabbed her pink jacket off the couch "What's your plan Charlie May?"

Charlie just smiled softly reaching out for her friend's hand. "There is no plan."

The air was cool and crisp, the empty swings and benches illuminated by the soft glow of streetlights. A phone sat atop a colorful pile of jackets playing quiet pop music from a playlist called "Night Time Vibez"

Oliver and Charlie had climbed to the top of the monkey bars, their legs swinging casually, the wind blowing their hair and carrying their laughter as they reminisced over the game of "floor is lava" the group played moments ago, where Oliver just about ate dirt trying to jump from structure to structure.

The rhythmic creaking of the swing chains punctuated the night air, the sounds of laughter and the faint music seemed far away to Amelie as she gently swung in the air. With each upward swing, the chains creaked softly, and a comfortable lurch settled in her stomach. At the top, with her eyes closed, the world below seemed distant, and for a moment, she felt weightless. A warm sense of calm washed over her as the swing drifted back down, her brain had promptly shut off, now focusing only on the rhythm of the swing.

Oliver settled into the peaceful sounds of the swing's chains and the music he had played. He looked over at Charlie and felt his breath catch in his throat. She wasn't watching him, but she seemed entranced with the moment. It was peaceful, just the three of them, the soft gentle breeze and the music. She looked peaceful. "Charlie?"

She turned her head to look at him addressing her name with a soft hum.

He stared at her not having a clue what he wanted to say. He blinked and looked ahead of him "This was a good idea. Coming to the park, it's nice out."

"Yeah well," She shrugs softly "I was trying to be spontaneous. I wouldn't typically opt to leave the house past 10."

Oliver chuckled proudly "Live out of choice, not habit" He mused "That's what my mother always said."

The group decided to call it a night at Oliver's house. They watched a comedy movie and pretended that they were in English class looking for the deeper meanings, laughing as they joked that their English teacher would be so proud of them.

Now the tv was turned off and the only noise was the soft hum of the fan that Oliver needed to fall asleep. Oliver was lying on his back on the blanket pallet he made, he stared at the ceiling before looking over at Charlie who had fallen asleep on the couch before the end of the movie. He didn't have the heart to wake her, he simply covered her with a blanket and made sure to stay silent while getting everything ready for bed.

"Oliver, you awake?" Amelie's soft voice came from the other couch.

"Yeah, you need something?"

Amelie was quiet for a moment "I'm not a hater, you know, about love and stuff?"

"What do you mean?" The question flowed out with a curious tone, light and easy. His voice held a hint of interest, but never judgment.

"I mean I like love. Like your mom and dad are cute, Skylar and Aaron aren't half bad. Man, even my parents have their good moments," She paused. "I think about Lily and Grayson sometimes. What they could've had if things went differently."

He started to understand that Amelie had been thinking back to their different perspectives of the book they were reading in English. "Yeah, they seemed to really love each other."

Amelie listened to the hum of the fan. "I don't love anything that much, I just sacrifice. But I want to" Even though Oliver had never once judged her, she didn't want to give him the opportunity to question her further. Slowly she turned onto her side to face Oliver better. The dim glow of the moon filtered through the window, casting soft shadows across the room. She could vaguely see Oliver on the floor, blanket half-draped over him. "When are you going to tell her?"

Caught off guard by the unexpected question, he started searching for words that escaped him, leaving him speechless, lips parted as he struggled to process. It was a split second of vulnerability, his usual composure slipping away, which Amelie was slightly proud to shake him from.

"What do you mean?" he muttered.

"You know exactly what I mean, Knight" She chuckled "You like her, and you haven't told her."

"She has a lot going on."

Amelie snorted "When will she not have a lot going on." She continued "Listen, I think you might be the only other person who cares about Charlie as much as I do, and honestly, I don't think anyone else gets her like you would."

"You love Charlie" He reminds her after a moment. He did not agree that Amelie didn't love anything that much.

Amelie hums softly "I'm not what she needs."

She stayed quiet for a moment to let the words sit with him before she spoke again "I think you are the only one in our group who seems so carefree about things. You're not trying to change anything."

He chuckled softly "I thought you didn't like it when the guy came to save the girl?"

"You're not saving her. It's not some contest" She points out "You're just there along for the ride."

Oliver thought about it and that was true, he never wanted to be the hero in Charlie's story. She didn't need him to save her, she didn't need saving. But he would be happy to be along for the ride.

Chapter 31

Just Not Here

"Amelie Henderson" The principal stood at the podium on stage, microphone in hand. Her voice rang clear announcing each name with pride.

Charlie stood in line with the other graduates, her eyes followed Amelie as she walked across the stage to get her diploma and shake the hands of the school's administrators. Charlie, along with the other students, clapped and cheered for her.

Quickly her eyes went to the audience and saw Amelie's father standing up from his seat in the bleachers cheering loudly for his daughter, his wife had stayed sitting but was clapping as well. A row in front of them sat Oliver's parents who also clapped, and his older brother who yelled loudly for Amelie.

Charlie clapped for the other names called but was really tuning them out until it was Oliver and her turn. Her eyes scanned the crowd again, it not taking long before she saw her uncle Aaron sitting to the right of Oliver's family. She was a bit surprised to see Skylar sitting next to him, with all of the kids.

"Oliver Knight." The principal called out.

Charlie looked back at the stage and clapped for him loudly, she cheered just like she did for Amelie and watched him as he walked across the stage, shook hands, and grabbed his diploma.

Her eyes went back to the audience in time to see his parents and his three brothers standing and cheering for him. His older two whooped and hollered, the youngest sitting on top of the eldest's shoulders, also clapping for his brother.

Charlie wondered how it felt to stand on that stage and have your whole family cheer for your accomplishments. She was grateful for Aaron being there, and sure Skylar was there but like the rest of the crowd, she only cheered because it was what was expected.

As she moved forward in the line her thoughts drifted to her mom, she hoped she was proud of her. Would she be one of those moms that brought air horns, or one of those weird signs with Charlie's face on it? Would she be the parent to stay sitting in her chair or would she be standing making her presence known?

She thought about Ms. Vivian and how she missed her too. She had kind of hoped that she would at least be here for this. Ms. Vivian was the closest one she had to a mother figure, and it did sting a bit when she had moved away, but Charlie couldn't be upset with her, knowing that the older woman needed her own adventure too.

She liked to imagine that both her mother and Ms. Vivian would be proud of her for walking across this stage and completing this part of her life. With everything she went through, she continued to grow and take steps in the right direction of who her mother wanted her to be, who Ms. Vivian thought she could be. Who she wanted to be.

She was learning about her potential. She was strong and ever-growing. She continued to remind herself that even the smallest beginnings could lead to great achievements. This was a great achievement, having her friends was a great achievement, and getting into the college she wanted was a great achievement.

"Charlie May." The principal's voice ranged out over the microphone.

Charlie walked up the ramp and onto the stage, her thoughts simply about keeping one foot in front of the other. She smiled and shook her principal's hand before taking her diploma. She turned to look at the crowd and smiled. The audience seemed a lot louder once she was on stage, her eyes swept through the crowd before landing on her uncle Aaron.

Aaron stood up from his seat and was cheering and whistling. Victor was clapping wildly. Oliver's parents and brothers were screaming and hollering as well, Amelie's father was shouting out her name like he had for Amelie. Even Skylar was clapping.

She glanced down at the crowd and caught a glimpse of Amelie and Oliver cheering loudly, clapping with their hands above their heads.

Overcome with emotions, Charlie managed to walk off stage and back to her seat.

This was a great achievement.

After all the graduation photos were taken and everyone went back to the Knight's house for a graduation party with pizza and ice cream, the group spent some time together knowing that tomorrow Amelie would be moving. They sat and talked about old memories while one of their favorite movies played in the background.

It was hard for Charlie not to be emotional when reminiscing, knowing that when tomorrow came part of her group would be gone. She didn't cry but came close a few times, but Amelie always stopped her.

"If you cry, I'll cry," She told her before playfully grinning "And we only want Oliver to cry."

"Ah, I'm going to miss being bullied" Oliver jokingly wiped a tear from his eye.

Charlie laughed and found it a bit easier to keep it together. She did it for Amelie, knowing that Amelie did not like to cry.

Charlie now sat in the passenger seat of Amelie's noisy 2007 GT Mustang. The two had tried for a good five minutes to get the Bluetooth connected before deciding to sit in silence. Charlie was worried that the roar of the car's engine would wake the neighbors, Amelie must have had the same thought because she rolled down the windows and turned the car off.

Charlie relaxed in her seat as cool air filled the car. "We did it." She said after the long moment of silence

"Of course, we did." Amelie had turned to look at Charlie "I always knew we would. Had some doubts about Oliver from time to time though."

Charlie laughed a bit before turning to face her "He made the group interesting though, at least give him that" The three of them had been together for years so there was never a dull moment. "Do you remember that night we were walking back to my house from the pool, and we heard some kind of screeching noise in the distance. You were convinced it was Oliver."

Amelie laughed "Yes! Dude, I don't think I have ever run away so fast. I am still convinced to this day that it was him, and that he got back to the house before we did."

"That was nothing compared to that time when I walked into your room, and you scared me so bad because you were standing on a chair eating popcorn and when you saw me you made some kind of gremlin noise." Charlie erupted into laughter midway through the story, her head tilting back as she relived that moment.

"Oh god." Amelie mumbled laughing with her "You scared me! I forgot you were coming over and you just busted into my room!"

Amelie laughing only made Charlie laugh harder, trying to catch her breath, but the laughter kept coming. "I scared you?! I'm not even sure that noise was human!"

"I could not make that noise again if I tried!"

The two busted out laughing so hard that their stomachs began to ache, and they doubled over. Every time one of them attempted to speak, it only triggered another fit of giggles. The girls continued to laugh and talk over memories and future promises.

"Remember me when you're super famous and throwing events for celebrities." Charlie joked.

"I'll make sure to get you an invitation to every party," She grinned "Only VIP treatment for my best girl"

As their conversation began to wind down, Charlie noticed that the clock on the radio dash showed 2:30 a.m. and yet she couldn't bring herself to get out of the car, knowing that she wouldn't be able to simply text Amelie to come over anymore.

"Charlie, you have to promise me something."

"What?"

"Promise me you will continue to live the life that you want. I want you to remember that you deserve better than this."

Only once Charlie finally tore her eyes away from the clock to look at Amelie, then did it hit her that she wasn't going to have her best friend by her side come morning time. The thought of having to do things without Amelie only made her want to crawl back to the familiar more. But now was the time to be brave. This was where her story began.

Charlie knew she needed to leave. She needed to get some sleep and Amelie needed to get home for her long day tomorrow. With a small breath, Charlie broke the silence, knowing that goodbye was coming. "We're acting like we'll never see each other again," she said while opening the door.

Charlie stood there, in the empty street, while Amelie spoke, almost laughing. "But we will, just not here"

Chapter 32

Welcome To Grand Fayword

Sitting three feet from Vivian's old house, Charlie gazed down the winding road lined by rows of towering trees. In the distance, she could see the familiar weathered sign, "Welcome to Grand Fayword!"

Slowly, she reached out her hand out to feel the static-like feeling against her skin. "In all the books we read and the movies we consume, once the character learns their lesson their life drastically changes" Her voice was soft as she kept her hand against the buzzing forcefield.

With a gentle touch, Oliver reached out, wrapping his fingers around Charlie's wrist and slowly pulling her hand away from the barrier. He brought her hand down and rested it between them before intertwining their fingers. He only hummed softly in response to her statement.

"I know I should be upset that it doesn't work that way," Charlie glanced down at their hands "But I've learned to make the most out of my situation."

Charlie still had a lot of unanswered questions and uncertainty about what she wanted out of life. She missed her mother and Ms. Vivian and was still very curious about Grayson. But she was going to have to figure out what she wanted her life to look like, and how to live it.

“What are you going to do when you get out of here?” Oliver spoke up softly.

“I tried not to think too hard about that” She hums softly “I suppose I’d go visit Ms. Vivian, after seeing Amelie of course.”

“You know where Vivian is?” He turned to look at her.

“She wrote it in this letter” Without letting go of his hand, she reached into her pocket and pulled out the letter that Vivian had written her. She carried it around on days when she needed a little reminder. “See”

Oliver carefully took the letter and tilted his head “Charlie, Vivian lives in New York. Written here is an address for a place in Evergreen Heights”

To Be Continued...